CRACKED SCREENS

MATTHEW A. GOODWIN

PART 1

CHAPTER 1

"You know what I miss?" Gibbs asked, breaking the silence.

Moss looked up at him, eyes burning. "What's that?"

"Remember those pressed peanut butter and jelly balls we got for lunch every day?" Gibbs' smile was sad. "They came in a three pack?"

Moss chuckled. "Right, with the little BurbBud guy on the packaging. I forgot about those. You really *did* love them."

"Well, they were really good," Gibbs argued, only half-jokingly. "I mean, by burb standards."

"They were so gross," Issy put in. Sitting next to Moss, she had been lost in thought but this conversation was enough to bring her back to the moment.

Gibbs scoffed. "You just don't like peanuts. That doesn't make them gross."

"Oh, puh-lease," Issy said, rolling her eyes. "I doubt there was a peanut within a thousand kilometers of those balls."

"Point being," Gibbs said, ignoring her, "they were delicious."

"Moss, my darling, love of my life, light of my heart, help me out here," Issy pleaded, batting her eyelashes.

A guilty expression crossed his face. "I mean, I didn't hate them," he said meekly.

Issy's mouth fell open. "You are telling me that you grew up eating my dad's makhni and you still thought that other crap was palatable?" She seemed genuinely shocked by this revelation.

"Know what I grew up eating?" Ynna interrupted by way of saving Moss.

Gibbs rolled his eyes theatrically. "Caviar cereal?" he asked with a broad grin.

Issy chuckled. "Champagne juice boxes?"

Moss tried to come up with something clever but he couldn't.

"Black truffle string cheese?" Gibbs barked a laugh at his own joke and Issy was grinning ear to ear.

"You know what?" Ynna pointed a finger seriously for a moment and then grinned. "You guys aren't that far off."

Moss looked up at her, her hair microdyed black to match her outfit. "Really?"

"Yeah, legit," she said. "I was sent to elementary university with toasted crackers and a tin of foie gras."

They all chuckled at that.

Patchwork poked his head through a curtain into the little room. "Moss, you ready?"

Moss swallowed hard and nodded. Gibbs clapped a hand on his shoulder and Issy squeezed the hand she was holding. He stood and Ynna smiled sadly at him.

"You got this," Ynna told him with a wink.

He stepped through the curtain and the rest followed behind, walking down the aisle that bisected all the pews. They were using the dilapidated remains of a temple, the broken stained glass providing an eerie light. The heavy rain dripped and leaked, filling the room with cold and damp. It felt fitting.

A neon billboard, some ad for a long-extinct beer, had been dragged in and attached to a little generator to provide light. This event had to be clandestine. As Moss walked past the leaders of the various crews from around the city, he appreciated the need for secrecy. He had even been told that there had never been this many of them together at once. But things had changed. Now, they all needed to work together for the betterment of the city's citizens.

Moss sat in the front row and his friends sat bedside. Jo, Patchwork's mom and one of Sandra's few friends, nodded at them and stepped onto the low stage with the aging podium. Her face was stoic but Moss knew she was upset. The crumpled slip of paper in her hand trembled and her eyes were swollen. She wore a black leather vest, black jeans and black boots. Her long dreadlocks were pulled back into a bundle under a cowboy hat.

As she stepped before the assembled crowd, she looked down at the paper, then up at the room.

"Sandra would have hated this," she choked out. Everyone laughed and Moss nodded, a tear rolling down his cheek. "Everyone in this room knew the woman who brought us together today, so I won't tell you who she was and I won't mince words.

"She was tough sumbitch, she was a ball-buster and a hero. She made you want to follow her into war and she made you want to punch her in the face."

Another round of laughter and Moss tried to blink away the memory of her in her final moments.

"Most of the people in this room are united by a cause and that cause wouldn't exist without Sandra. She started something much bigger than herself and lived long enough to see it take shape. If any of us can feel that way on our final days on this plant, we can count ourselves lucky."

She looked to Moss. "And now, her grandson will say a few words…" a little smile crossed her lips . . . "*then* you can drink."

The room chuckled as Moss stood, feeling the hands of support as he moved toward the little stage. Jo hugged him deeply and his mind flashed to that night, to the last time he saw his grandmother alive. Choking down tears, he left the embrace and stepped to the podium. A book lay open in front of him, the pages dusty and wilted. He didn't recognize the language.

He looked up to the gathering. It was remarkable.

For as hard a woman as she was, she really had brought people together — her soldiers in the war, her revolutionaries in the cause. She had become hardened and indifferent, even lost, since leaving Carcer City; but she had led a meaningful life and that made her grandson happy.

Moss knew what he had to do now. Clearing his throat, he looked to all the awaiting eyes.

"Voltaire once said, 'history is filled with the sound of silken slippers going downstairs and wooden shoes coming up,' and everyone in this room followed the sound of Grandma's wooden shoes," he said, his voice steady. "She died in the shadow of a fallen tyrant. Carcer is gone. The people who imprisoned and tortured Sandra have been forced from this city by us. By every person in this room. If you are celebrating her life, she also celebrated you for helping her to thrust the yoke of her captors from the shoulders of this great city."

Moss could feel the energy changing in the room. He could feel people getting excited about their accomplishments.

"She was always proud to work alongside each and every one of you, even if she didn't show it, and I am proud to continue her legacy. Carcer may be gone, but there is still much work to do. We have rid the city of one mega but it is time we force them all to their knees, to show them what a power the people of this world can be.

"We are all here to honor the memory of a freedom fighter and there is no greater honor than to pick up the mantle and continue the fight!" he cheered and the room erupted. Gone was the somber mood, replaced with an electric energy.

Moss pulled a flask from his pocket and held it aloft. "To Sandra!" he cried.

"To Sandra!" echoed back as he saw her eyes staring up at him one last time. He felt a jolt, like someone knocking on the door of his brain.

Patchwork, who had been standing to the side with his mother as everyone began to get up and make their way to the makeshift bar in the corner of the room, hurried over to Moss.

"The program?" he asked. Moss knew Patch had seen his reaction to it enough times to tell.

"Not sure," Moss answered honestly. He looked Patchwork in the eyes. When they had met, he had seemed so youthful; but now, he was as grizzled as the rest of them. "I haven't had any incidents with the program since I started taking the pills but I feel like, I don't know, with everything going on and ever since Arthur Smith was in there…" he trailed off and Patch simply nodded.

"Heard," he said. "Maybe it's time for a scan. I know ThutoCo uses off-world materials that aren't supposed to rust or break down, but maybe it's worth looking into."

Moss let out a grim chuckle. "As if the idea of our enemies hacking my brain wasn't bad enough, now I have to worry about battery acid or some shit in my head?"

"Funny how they never mention the physical realities of all these cybernetics during the sales pitch," Patch joked.

"Yeah," Moss said. "Real fucking funny. I have to go chat," Moss added as he caught Mayor LeBeau's eye. Patchwork slapped him on the back and Moss jumped down from the stage. People muttered words of condolence as he moved but he paid them little mind.

He approached the mayor he had helped get elected. They were perfectly attired for the occasion. They wore a black suit with faux fur collar; large, layered frills sticking out from the sleeves; and a cascading black skirt with long strings of shimmering beads.

"Mayor," Moss said with a smile as the mayor's assistant made herself scarce.

"Mister Moss," Persimmon said with a somber expression. "Sorry for your loss."

Moss sighed. "Her death is a loss for all of us."

"Quite right," they agreed.

"How is life without Carcer?" Moss asked. "I'm getting mixed reports."

"We are having mixed results," LeBeau said, and Moss knew he had hit a nerve. "Carcer was a terrible option but change is painful. We have your friends, those bounty hunters and other assorted ruffians, helping but we are still in the process of establishing a civic protection force. In addition, I have to craft laws that both serve the people *and* function for them. Everyone in this city has known only policing-for-pay their entire lives and many are not thrilled about the idea of state police. This change requires an upheaval of the entire system, and though the people want change, they do not want to have to change."

Moss ran his hands down his face. "Sure, that makes sense," he said. "Nothing can ever be easy."

Persimmon smiled. "Nothing worth doing, no."

Moss let his attention wander, looking across the room at Issy and wishing, as he often did these days, that he could just run off with her.

"Also," the mayor said in a hushed tone. "There have been some attacks on mutual friends and backers. Known associates have been killed without a trace."

"Without a trace?" Moss asked, assuming the mayor was being hyperbolic. "Think it's ThutoCo?"

"They may be at the top, but the list is long," Persimmon said. They draped an arm over Moss's shoulder, pulling him in close. The mayor smelled good, as always. Moss was used to spending time with people for whom daily showers were a luxury. "We need to sort this before our friends begin to think it's not worth it."

Moss blew a bit of fur off his face. "I understand."

"Do more than understand," Persimmon warned. "I know your fire has as many irons as mine, but neither of us will survive what comes next without friends."

"I understand," he said again, looking right into the mayor's tired but sharp eyes. "Call us when you hear anything about another attack."

Persimmon narrowed their eyes. "I *have* been calling."

"I'll get the details from Seti," he said, pointing in her direction. "Not trying to excuse myself here, but we have been dealing with quite a mound of shit," Moss said, nodding toward the stage.

Persimmon's face grew kind, their perfectly applied makeup shimmering in the low light. "I know. We are all up to our ears in shit and it's hard not to try and shovel a bit in other directions. I'm sorry. How are you doing with all this?"

Moss considered the question. It felt like so much had changed so quickly. After they had gotten Persimmon elected, Belle had been hacked by one of the megas in retaliation and killed their pilot, Anders. Sandra had immediately killed Zip Thud for the actions of his android girlfriend. Gibbs and Ynna had threatened to leave the crew because of Sandra, who had then died the night of their wedding. Meanwhile, Steampuck had infiltrated the Carcer Corporation before assaulting the Arthur Smith, the head of ThutoCo. And then all the major changes were also happening throughout the city because of the new mayor. Just the thought of it all threatened to crush Moss's brain.

"I am doing as well as I can," he said.

The mayor let out a laugh. "One hell of a political answer. You don't have to tell me," they said before adding, "as long as you are telling someone."

Moss nodded. "Thank you for coming."

"It was a pleasure," they said. "She was a true revolutionary."

"That she was," Moss agreed and they shook hands. Moss turned to look around the room. So many conversations required his attention, but all he wanted to do was go talk to Issy. She stood in a corner with a few of her former BurbSec coworkers, who were now their agents inside ThutoCo.

"Talk soon," Persimmon said and moved to speak with their assistant who was standing over by the bar.

Detritus Two had hijacked a truck full of real liquor (rather than the usual synth stuff they were all so accustomed to drinking) as a gesture of honor. They had brought with them a little plastic table with bent metal legs and, from there, they were serving drinks. More accurately, they were handing out bottles.

It was quite a moment. When Moss first arrived in the city, he had been told that the crews never came together and now he was witnessing the second such gathering. The first time, only a handful of the crews had shown up to save Moss from ThutoCo; but this time, everyone was here. Now that people were up and milling about, the room seemed packed.

Normally, he would have felt like a sitting duck with all the crews assembled. But with Carcer gone, he felt almost safe. Almost.

He saw Seti looking at him, her bizarre, telescoping cylindrical eyes pointing in his direction. They pushed through the people and met next to a crumbling pillar.

"Ask and ye shall receive," he told her.

"What's that?" she asked in her Australian accent, pushing her blond hair behind her ears.

"Nothing," he said. "I was just saying that I should catch up with you."

"Got that right," she said. "Saw you chatting to the mayor. They tell you we are in a fix?"

"Yes," Moss said. "Why didn't *you* tell me this?"

Moss could tell he hit a nerve as Seti's whole body seemed to shift in annoyance, her arms folding instantly and her leg repositioning outward toward him. He was two for two in annoying his allies the instant he walked over to them.

"I told Ynna, but I think she was trying to filter for you since you've been … busy …"

Moss didn't appreciate the implication. "Busy grieving."

"Either way, busy," Seti said.

Moss shook his head. "We have a problem?"

"For fuck's sake, Moss," Seti hissed. "No, *we* don't have a problem but I also don't appreciate you coming at me like I'm trying to keep information from you. I'm trying to help coordinate countless crews throughout a city of millions but, yeah, sorry you didn't get a memo."

"Right," Moss said. He never really thought about all Seti did for them. "Sorry."

"Should be," Seti sighed. "She meant a lot to me, too, you know."

"Of course," Moss said. That was something he had also come to appreciate since she had died. "You want to tell me?" he asked. "It helps to hear."

Seti shifted, her black dress wafting gently.

"I was brought to the states at gunpoint, the intended bride of a muckety-muck at D2E; that horrible, evil, giant entertainment conglomerate. My parents sold me to feed their Mass Illusion addiction, same old sad sob. When I arrived, it turned out it wasn't just sex the bastard was after. He wanted to use me, too. Taught me a bunch of shit and did this to me." She tapped the cybernetics protruding from her face. "He had gone mad. Reporting the news had sent him down a rabbit hole that ended in pure insanity. I spend my days chasing conspiracies and my nights chained to a bed.

"Finally started to hear chatter. Started to hear about some group of vigilantes. They were fighting back against all the systems that had landed me where I was. They were trying to cover their tracks, but they were old warriors and didn't know the first thing about it. So, I was able to break into their systems and reach out. Offered my services if they could free me."

She shrugged in a the-rest-is-history sort of way but Moss wanted to know more. "And?"

She chuckled. "About what you would expect. They didn't run complex ops the way we do now. They kicked in the door, Sandra put a bullet in the man's face, and Burn burned the whole apartment down. By the time Crassun Emergency Services arrived, there wasn't fuck-all left."

"Sounds about right," Moss said. "It'll be hard to keep that spirit alive without them."

Seti shrugged. "They live on in her," she said, nodding in the direction of Ynna.

Moss nodded slowly. "Right, in her."

CHAPTER 2

"Can we talk?" Moss asked Ynna, who screwed up her face as she turned to him.

"Sure," she said, giving a little wave to the people with whom she had been speaking and following Moss back to his spot by the pillar. The ancient cement was cracked, chunks littering the floor. Within, exposed rebar was beginning to rust as plants took root and reclaimed the spot. "How you doing?" she asked with a crooked smile. "The speech really worked."

"Thanks," Moss said and he looked her right in the eye. "Have you been keeping stuff off my plate?"

Ynna guffawed, the sound of her laugh echoing through the building, turning some heads. She looked at him in shock.

"Yeah, man, I filter a whole bunch of shit. Even before Sandra died, I was half running this show. You got your panties in a wad because I kept something from you? You're in for a rude awakening tomorrow when we go on our honeymoon. You'll see how much I have to sift through. Then we will see how pissy you feel." She slapped him on the shoulder, rolled her eyes and asked, "Was that it?"

Moss felt like an idiot so he tried to cover. "Also wanted to know how you are doing, given everything?"

She shook her head. "I'm all over the place. Gibbs is frayed too, you know. Poor sack has to take care of both you and me, you know? Plus, like, his best friend's grandma and his wife's surrogate mother died on his wedding day. So, that puts a damper on everything …"

"Right, sure," Moss said. "Everything feels so fucked now. This was supposed to be our time but instead . . " he trailed off, shaking his head.

"We will get it back," Ynna said, reaching out and squeezing his arm. "We always do."

"A week away should help," Moss noted with a somber smile.

"Here's hoping," she said, raising her glass and taking a drink. "I'm a little worried Gibbs is going to be more concerned with the scenery than with this scenery," she made a sweeping gesture toward her body. Moss opened his mouth to try and formulate some response on the fly but Ynna cut him off. "Oh, also, that reminds me, I met with the Scubas last night."

"Right, of course," Moss said, pulling the flask from his jacket and taking a quick swig. "How are they doing?"

"Good," Ynna said. "LeBeau got them situated with some other MonoGoders in Wallburg. They are happy but seem a bit overwhelmed. Like, these people have been living out in The Betweens for generations and now they are supposed to just figure out life in the city."

Moss chuckled. "Yeah, the city can be a rude awakening."

"Got that right," Ynna nodded and a broad grin crossed her face. "Ready for the bombshell that's not really a bombshell?"

"It's not actually toxic out there?" Moss asked with an eyebrow raised.

Ynna punched him in the arm. "How did you know?"

"Lots of little things," Moss told her. "But mostly it was the mere fact that ThutoCo needed the Scubas to even exist. The more I thought about it, the more it just seemed like a distraction. The company had this vague looming threat of these wild people. Plus, their name was just so on the nose and a constant reminder of how it was 'toxic' out there."

"Right!" Ynna exclaimed.

"Like, you would hear people make claims that maybe it was all a lie or whatever, but then a new video of a Scuba getting infected would surface. Guessing that is all some CGI bullshit?"

Ynna's face grew dark. "Worse," she said. "ThutoCo would set them up from time to time. Draw them into some zone they would reinfect ahead of time and then fire precision shots to blast the Scuba's masks off. *Those* are the videos you would see. They have proof, though. The video evidence and documentation."

Moss remembered sitting in his hex, getting the feed and watching as the spores infected the Scubas, turning them into mindless monsters. "I, wow, I mean, fuck," he muttered. "These people have had it worse than most."

"And most have it pretty bad," Ynna added.

"So, what's next?"

Ynna gave him a half-smile. "That's gonna be on you, bossman."

"You're only gone a week."

Ynna rolled her eyes. "Sure, but if you are stepping into Sandra's place, you need to, you know, actually do it. You think I'm gonna run this shit while you bask in the glory, you've got another think coming."

"It's not like that," Moss said.

"No," Ynna said seriously. "You don't *want* it to be like that."

15

"But . . ." Moss said and planned to say more but Ynna held up her metal hand.

"Look, man, I know you have a good heart and you try really hard, but you are also overwhelmed by shit. You have a broken-ass program in your head and worry you are going to be hacked; your family lied to you and have been behind the eight-ball since you left the burbs. I get all that. But that shit means you only have enough RAM for so many things. That's going to have to change. I'm not going to be your woman behind the scenes, doing all the work while you lead the revolution."

As she reiterated the point, Moss's instinct was to argue, to say it wasn't true, but she was right. She was right about all of it. He had to step up, learn to be the leader he claimed to be. "You're right," he admitted.

A broad grin crossed her face. "Think you could teach your friend that expression?"

"Wasn't able to in the years before we met you," Moss said with a smirk. "Still don't want to tell me where you guys are going tomorrow?"

Ynna shook her head. "Better you don't know."

"ThutoCo captures and tortures me, I'm pretty sure you are going to be the last thing on their mind," Moss said dryly.

"Even still," she said. "We will show you pics when we get back."

"Of the 'scenery?'" Moss asked with a wink.

"Oh, soooo hilarious," she said in an unidentifiable 'fancy' accent.

"Ynna," Moss said as she turned to rejoin Gibbs. "I'm sorry, I don't mean to take advantage of you or anything."

"I know," she smiled. "So prove it."

"What do I need to do?"

After Ynna had listed all the various things she had going on, Moss finally made his way over to Issy. She was talking to Judy and trying to keep the mood light, but Moss could tell that Judy was still on the verge. They had lost so much. They had gone rogue after their partner, Stan, had been killed in Carcer City, and the loss of so many more was clearly taking a toll. Judy had always believed in the fight, but the relentless loss hit them hard.

"That was a nice speech," Judy said. "Good use of the platform."

Moss shrugged. "Thanks." He could tell that Issy wanted to grab him and hold him, but she was not going to rub their affection in Judy's face. "We've got trouble," he told them.

"What else is new?" Judy asked with a dark laugh.

"This time it's not us they are after, it's our friends," Moss said. "Those friends with deep pockets."

"Oh, shit," Judy said.

"Got that right," Moss agreed. "So, now we have to figure out who is behind it and stop them before our funding all dries up."

"More than that, we should also figure out how, whoever this is, knows who our friends are," Issy said.

Judy turned to scan the room. "Think we've got a leak?"

Moss sighed. "Hadn't even considered that."

"Well, you were an engineer, not a security officer," Issy noted. "It was my job to think that way."

"Right," Moss said, letting his eyes wander over all the faces— familiar and not. "Speaking of my old life," he said, and told them what Ynna had just explained about the Scubas.

"Fuck," Judy snarled. "ThutoCo are just the worst."

"Oh, don't play it like our old employer is worse than yours," Moss said, nudging Judy with his elbow.

"Don't get me wrong, Carcer is evil, too; but this is just an extra special blend," Judy said. "To take people whose only crime was faith and forcing them to live out in the wasteland to sell the world on their lies, that's some evil shit."

"I don't get it," Issy said quietly. "I'm not apologizing for it or anything, but I just don't understand why ThutoCo is even doing it."

"Think everyone would want to stay in the cities if they knew the land outside was inhabitable?" Judy asked, as though trying to cover up their judgement.

"Well, no, but so what?" Issy asked, her frustration in not being able to see it becoming evident. "I mean, so what if people know?"

Moss watched Judy's face contort. "So people would leave the cities and take back the planet. ThutoCo has clear-cut most of the continent to make space for solar panels or prophet root fields. You think they have that land legally? Think they have the manpower to protect it if all the poor people from all the cities leave?"

"Oh," Issy said, her eyes going wide. "And the Scubas have proof?"

"Yes," Moss said.

Issy was excited now. "We have to let people know; we have to get the word out."

Moss smiled. "That we do."

"You have a plan for that?" she asked, looking like she was going to vibrate off the face of the earth.

"No," Moss admitted before justifying, "I literally only just learned this a minute ago."

"Can't do it like we normally do," Judy said, running their thumb along one of the buttons on their suit jacket to scrape off a little dirt. They, like everyone else, wore all black but had adorned their suit with lengths of silver chains connecting random parts of the suit together like exposed mechanical veins. Judy hardly ever dressed up, preferring functional clothes that they didn't mind getting covered in grease or scorch marks.

"Why's that?" Moss asked. He really wanted to know. He hadn't really given it much thought but was sure Judy would have a point.

"Because," they sighed, "we use the internet to disseminate all this information, but also disinformation. People are so fucking jaded that they believe the most insane shit but doubt true horrors. We need to get this out in some way that people will have to confront it. We probably have to use D2E."

"D2E?" Moss asked, really surprised. "No one trusts the traditional media."

Judy laughed. "No, everyone claims to distrust the news media, but they all have it on in the background all day long, letting it seep into their brain. So, while they get their extra crazy online, they get the news they love to doubt from the source."

Moss took another swig from his flask and sighed as though he could push out the weight of the world. "You have any friends at D2E?" he asked, only half-joking.

"You should ask Seti if we have any friends on the inside," Judy said, just as an old investigator they knew waved their way. They turned to Issy. "Take care of him," Judy said and turned back to Moss. "We will see it done... for her."

Moss smiled. "Thanks, Jude," he said. "But also, for Stan."

"He woulda loved to see you now," they said, squeezing Moss's hand before excusing themselves with a nod.

Issy looked at Moss with big, caring eyes. He knew she was worried about him. "You know my father really wanted to be here," she said.

"I know. It just wasn't worth the risk."

"Oh, no, I get it," she said. "I actually didn't want him here, but he just wanted you to know that he's thinking about you."

"That's sweet," Moss said, and he meant it. Vihaan had always taken such good care of him growing up and was one of the only reasons he was even alive today. "I would like to go visit."

"Let's!" Issy said so enthusiastically that her joy echoed around the room.

Moss smiled at her. Little moments like that were what he lived for. All the other stuff was just noise when she smiled.

"Yeah, let's," he said and laced his fingers through hers. She smiled up at him, masking her fear.

"Sounds like we have a lot to deal with," Issy said.

"With Gibbs and Ynna gone for a week, we will have a lot to do."

"At least we will be doing it together."

He kissed her softly and the world fell away. All the cybernetically enhanced rebels drinking in celebration of his grandmother disappeared.

Then he felt it again. Like an ice pick to the head.

Something was wrong and he knew it, but he pulled away and smiled at Issy.

PART 2

CHAPTER 3

"I was so sorry to hear of your loss," Vihaan told Moss, putting a hand on his shoulder.

"Thanks," Moss said, clapping his own hand on top of the man's.

Vihaan looked so much older than he had only a few years early. They had seen one another over video but looking at him now Moss could see the ravages of time and stress. The lines in his face were deep and sorrowful and the gray that once peppered his hair had now taken over, leaving only little indicative strands of his once-dark mane.

The restaurant he had bought was nice and, to Moss's great joy, full of patrons. It was on the fiftieth floor of a building in a part of the city called Rises where all the businesses were built on platforms jutting out from the sides of former apartments. The buildings had been built close together to accommodate the growing population, and bridges of found metal and cabling now connected the high rises to one another. Streets of ramshackle scaffolding attached businesses that were advertised by bright holoprojections competing for attention.

Moss and Issy were out on the balcony, surrounded by activity and bright lights that made it hard to remember it was night. People would look through the plastic windows that divided them from the street and make hushed comments to one another about how good the food looked. A few even came in.

"Your father spoke of her highly," Vihaan said with a smile.

Moss cocked his head. "Is that so?"

Vihaan laughed knowingly. "Perhaps not always."

"Tell me more," Moss said and Issy's father pulled a chair from one of the other tables and set it next to theirs, taking a small rip of a samosa from Issy's plate and popping it in his mouth before continuing. "Listen, I know we all think of our parents in a certain way, a rarified way, but they are people, same as us," he said thoughtfully. "Your father loved his mother but it was also a fraught relationship. He had the same goals as she but he never approved of her tactics. He wanted to outwit the enemy and she wanted nothing more than to kill them.

"As you would think, this caused many problems for them, especially since your father was trying to keep you safe and his ... other life ... separate. But this is all beside the point. They did love one another and he always was grateful to her."

Moss smiled to hear that. He had known his parents, who they really were, so little that it was nice to think of them as real people. The program in his mind with the AI construct of his father had given him a glimpse but this was more real. The real man who Vihaan had actually known.

"My father and my grandmother just seem so different from one another," Moss said.

Vihaan smiled and dipped his finger into the small silver bowl with Issy's palak but before he could speak, Issy blurted, "Go make your own!"

He smiled as he took the green sauce into his mouth. "Food is better when shared with family."

"Food is best when eaten," she said, pulling her dishes away, but her father plucked up her fork and stuck it in her paneer. She gasped in mock offense as he ate her cheese with a big grin. "Ugh," she groaned, getting up from the table. "I'll go get more for myself."

"Thank you, daughter," Vihaan said, unable to contain his amusement. Turning to Moss, he asked, "You plan to marry her?"

Nearly choking on his korma, Moss sputtered, "Yes."

"Good," Vihaan said approvingly. "You must never hurt her. You know this, yes?"

"Yes," Moss said, wondering if the whole thing had been a ploy to get his daughter to leave the table.

"Remember, I was BurbSec for forty years. I could easily kick that pale little ass of yours," he said, pointing a threatening finger, and Moss noticed for the first time how strong Vihaan truly was.

Moss smiled. "I've got news for you: your daughter was also in BurbSec and could easily kick my ass too."

Vihaan smiled at that and, seeing Issy returning out of the corner of his eye, changed the subject. "How's the food, tonight?"

"If there is a better combination than your lamb korma and goat cheese naan, I don't want to know about it," Moss offered with a smile and Vihaan seemed to know that he was telling the truth. He had been saying it since he was a child and it had always been true.

"Happy to hear it, son," Vihaan said as he slid the bowl in front of himself while Issy rejoined them.

"Dad been threatening you?" Issy asked with a wink.

"Yes," Moss laughed, averting his eyes. He watched as an ancient man hoofed his way along the rickety path with a wrapped rug full of computer components on his back. As he groaned by, a sour smell wafted over to the table, and once again Moss was reminded why he spent his days in mortal peril rather than just snuggling with Issy.

Moss, he heard in his mind's ear.

His eyes flashed up to Issy. "We got something."

There has been another attack, Seti informed him. *Letting the mayor know but you could get there before anyone disturbs the scene if you go now.*

Moss stood, scooping up one big piece of lamb in the warm bread and jamming it in his mouth. Wishing he had waited until after speaking, he sputtered, "Another friend," and that was all it took. Issy was up in a moment too.

"Oh, how I miss that," Vihaan said wistfully.

Swallowing hard and gulping a sip of water, Moss looked at the older man and said, "I will happily trade."

Vihaan clapped him on the back and frowned. "Those days are behind me. Now, go," he said and then added in a hushed tone, "and remember what I told you."

As they walked out of the restaurant and toward the nearest taxi pad, Issy asked, "He said something like, 'keep her safe?'"

Moss laughed. "Yep."

"And you told him it's actually the other way round?"

"Pretty much," Moss said with a smile.

"Good boy."

They pushed through the crowds of people window shopping along the narrow path that groaned and creaked underfoot. A food truck floated next to the path and Moss wondered how he navigated between all the bridges and power lines. The man within screamed out an offer of ramen but they ignored him, making their way to the corner of the building.

A sheet metal circle on bending arms stuck out from the side with two Cosmic Winds cabs sitting atop. Both were painted off-yellow. One had a human cabby sitting in the driver's seat. He had bleached blond hair, wore an orange tank top and was smoking out the window. The other had a hard-plastic statue of an old-time cab driver in the front seat and they made their way toward that one without speaking. They hopped in and Moss fed the coordinates to the cab which took off immediately, rumbling off the pad before gliding away from the buildings.

Moss pulled out a little holoprojector and set it down. A display of the victim came across the translucent screen. A woman in her fifties, dressed in a flowing red dress with pearls wrapped around her neck and dark hair pinned and sprayed into waves, was displayed next to her information.

Moss didn't think that she even noticed she was doing it as Issy began to read aloud, "Meagan Thurman, one thousand and fifty-five. Works as a production manager at Gro4All, that company that prints chicken breasts." Issy turned to Moss. "I never think about all the people who help us, you know? This woman has some whole story about what happened to her and why she decided to risk her life to fund a rebellion. It's amazing."

"She died for it," Moss noted, turning to look out the window. Rain had started to fall and stripes of water streaked down the window, catching the reflection of the endless sea of buildings housing the endless sea of humanity.

"A lot of people are dying," Issy said. "It's relentless."

Moss nodded and slid closer to her, putting his arm over her shoulder. She put her hand on his knee. He smiled. "It's why we have to take time to appreciate these moments."

She looked up at him, her big, beautiful eyes reflecting the lights of the city. "I know. There are few moments more romantic than going from dinner with my father to a crime scene."

Moss huffed and rolled his eyes.

"What?" Issy laughed. "I'm just saying that I'm super turned on now."

"Shut up." Moss chuckled.

"I'm so wet for you," she whispered breathily, trying to keep from laughing.

Moss burst out laughing. "Oh, will you be quiet."

"I order you to be quiet!" they said in unison, doing an impression of Gibbs doing an impression of a movie.

Laughing, they embraced and held one another tightly as they approached the building.

It was gigantic.

As they moved closer, the sheer size of it became clear. Moss had seen such buildings from street level and from above, but as the cab descended he began to truly understand.

The landing pad was in good order and they told the cab to wait for them. The animatronic nodded jerkily in agreement as they stepped out into the rain.

As with most free spaces in the city, the roof had also been largely converted into housing. Not in any official capacity, but all around the landing pad were tents, lean-tos and various other forms of temporary housing. A few faces turned from bundled piles but no one moved as Moss and Issy stepped down onto the roof.

The cab took back off to hover nearby and the two made their way between the shanties, ignoring pleas for food and money. There was a large glowing blue door that protected the building itself. As they approached, a keypad beside the door crackled to life and then died, as did the door barrier.

Moss and Issy looked at one another in confusion before Seti chimed in, *I got you*.

"Not creepy at all," Issy joked aloud.

If you think there is a place in this city you can go where I, or anyone else for that matter, can't see you, I've got a bridge to sell you, Seti reminded them as they stepped from the rain into the stairwell. *Every twenty floors is a mall level with amenities. You'll want to avoid those places*, she told them. *Fewer eyes on you, the better.*

Right, Moss communicated. *Anything else?*

When Seti didn't answer, he figured she had moved on to another crew and he followed Issy down the stairs and into the open space at the bottom. The elevators into the building itself were on the far side of the little food court with stalls for various electronics, unlockables for the Mass Illusion VR worlds and cloned pets at its center. Tables encircled the stalls and the walls were lined with the food vendors. Moss saw some old standards with yellowed walls and peeling linoleum beside trendy new places serving the flavor-of-the-year until they went out of business and were replaced by the next fad.

Issy moved quickly but not too quickly. She grabbed Moss's hand, pulling him forward. "People have almost no interest in couples," Issy had once told him while using this same ploy to stay inconspicuous. Moss had come up with several counterarguments in his mind, of which he had suggested none. But no heads turned as they moved toward the elevator and selected the correct floor.

"What do you think we'll find?" Issy asked.

Moss shrugged. "I have no idea. The life of a person who spends their whole life working for the man in order to ferret a little money away to revolutionaries could be just about anything."

"I'm expecting a lot of those oversized white tee shirts with pictures of a bunch of animals and some trees with the moon in the background. You know the ones I mean?"

Moss felt a smile cross his lips. "I do," he chuckled as the elevator ground to a halt, the screen mounted onboard still chirping away as they stepped into the hall. There were apartment doors on both sides and the hall itself was so narrow that people would have to turn their bodies to avoid bumping shoulders while passing one another. "Yeesh," he said as they made their way down the fluorescent lighted corridor.

"Yeah," Issy agreed as they walked, looking down the hallway that seemed to stretch on forever. "Never thought I would miss the burbs…"

"That's just it, right," Moss said. "ThutoCo gave us just enough that we wouldn't notice being prisoners."

"Right, but they provided housing and amenities and paid us nearly nothing," Issy said. "These folks living here are presumably paid next to nothing at some job in the city and then take that money to pay whatever-fucking-landlord-corp for these coffin apartments. How's it different?"

Moss shook his head. "It isn't," he said. "That's precisely the point. It's different versions of the same shit. That's what we are going to change."

"Here's hoping," she said, looking over her shoulder with a smile before turning back to the hallway's endless sameness.

Moss was glad she didn't press him for what they would do if they managed to beat the corporations and change the world. The question had been haunting him recently. It had been a point of contention with his grandmother and now was something he needed to sort out.

After what felt like a year of walking, they finally reached the door. It was unfurnished with stickers or paint like so many of the others had been. They heard a sound coming from inside and their eyes locked.

"Shit," Moss said. "Someone got here first."

CHAPTER 4

The two pulled guns and readied themselves for what came next.

"Always has to be a firefight," Moss groused and pressed the button to open the door that Seti had unlocked in preparation for their arrival. As it slid aside, both of their mouths fell open just before a cat darted out.

Issy's head whipped to follow it. "Shit!"

"Going after it?" Moss asked but it was already out of sight through a cracked door or out a small window or into the vents.

Issy shook her head. "No," she said, "but I think cat-lady still counts as the shirt."

"Okay," Moss chuckled, turning to marvel at the apartment. "But I think this may cancel that out."

"Riiight," Issy agreed as they stepped into the hallway of the apartment, allowing the door to close behind them and the grass to crunch under their feet.

The apartment was like nothing Moss had ever seen. The grass that pressed down as they walked over it was real. Undoubtedly genetically modified to survive indoors, but it was real, planted in dirt set into the floor. All the walls were digital displays as in their old hexes, but photorealistic with a pixel count unlike anything he had ever seen. It showed a lush green vista with flowering cherry blossom trees, their petals dancing to the ground. Overhead, clouds moved slowly to blot out the sun just a bit.

Built into the walls and substituting for door frames were immaculate recreations of buildings from the era of feudal Japan. Strong wooden structures jutted from the walls and low tables sat on mats through low doorways. A bird trilled and fluttered from a tree and Moss couldn't tell if it was real or a recreation of some kind. Between the digital displays were actual structures and holoprojections. It all fooled the brain, making it hard to remember that this was a person's apartment.

They kept their weapons raised as they moved through the space although Moss knew the sound had come from the cat. In the distance, a digital farmer cupped his hands over his eyes and shouted a greeting as they made their way toward an arched doorway. A cloth hung down, split in the middle and emblazoned with an emblem. Pushing it aside, the space that would normally be the small living room was another room with bamboo mats lining a polished wooden floor. A table set with a ceramic tea pot and cups was at the center of the room surrounded by pillows. There was a shrine on one side of the room and a painting on the other.

"Television," Issy said loudly and the painting shimmered, revealing itself to be a hologram that became the TV. On screen was The Belting Chef, D2E's latest reality competition show in which contestants had to sing while preparing their dishes.

"How'd you know?" Moss asked.

"We are in my world now," she said with a wink.

Moss nodded. He had learned to do all the things necessary for this life but Issy had trained to investigate. While the problems that arose in the burbs were nothing like those out here in the urban world, she still knew what she was doing.

He watched her examine everything as she moved around the room. He stepped toward the shoji door at the rear of the room and slid it open. The sleeping area was small, little more than a bed roll beside some burned out candles.

How was she killed? Moss asked Seti.

There was a pause before he heard, *It was staged to look like a triad hit. My contact in the Sunset Side said there was no reason for her to have been a target. All the murders have been made to look like accidents or street violence, but scratching the surface makes it easy to see that it's not. Whoever is doing this cares enough about covering their tracks to fake it but not enough to make it believable.*

The screen turned to a picture of a crime scene taken by a drone. A woman lay dead in the street. Zooming in showed that she had been shot. The camera panned to display a business card lying in a nearby puddle. Seti zoomed in close.

It's from the Dragon Lounge, a known triad front. But evidence that easy to find is hardly evidence at all. They were probably just hoping anyone looking into it would start poking around in the wrong places.

They can't possibly think we are that stupid, Issy put in. *If they are hitting contributors, they know it's us who would be looking for them.*

"Unless they are contracted help," Moss said, his eyes turning as another holographic bird flitted in and landed on the floor, pecking for food.

You guys finding anything useful? Seti asked.

"No," Moss said. With all the problems he had with his chip, he always preferred verbal communication to neural since he knew Seti could hear him. She was watching, always watching. "Her apartment is quite something."

I see that, Seti said.

Both Moss and Issy's heads turned at the same time. Footsteps moving up the hall. Heavy and purposeful. Their eyes met and they nodded, readying their weapons before moving to hide. Neither wanted to get into a firefight if it could be avoided. Issy slid into a built-in wardrobe and Moss ducked back into the bedroom, closing the door and moving toward the bedroll.

As he moved the blankets to hide under, he heard the slight shift of floorboards, the tell-tale sign of a hidden compartment. He couldn't help but laugh. The hidden panel under the bed was so obvious, but he figured it was mostly for show. The woman hadn't expected to be gunned down and have her house turned upside down.

Moss could hear voices outside the door. They were faint, from a few rooms away and over the sound of wind in the tall grass, but he could tell he had a few moments before they were in.

I'll try to keep them out, Seti told him and Moss nodded, knowing there was a camera somewhere in the room. It was times like this that Moss truly understood how wired the world had become and how easy it was for someone to be watching you at every single moment.

Moss heard thumping on the door and frustrated grumblings. He pushed the bedroll out of the way and began to tap on the floor, looking for the particular panel. One plank shifted ever so slightly and Moss stuck in a finger, prying up the board. Inside was precisely what one would expect: some trinkets that undoubtedly had sentimental value, physically printed pictures, drug paraphernalia that most people just tended to leave lying around these days and what Moss had been looking for. A cash chip. While most people used paperless currency, cash chips were used when people wanted to move money without a trace. They had to be digitally scrubbed, but it was a smart way to get money to a clandestine organization without someone getting wise. Moss pocketed the chip and heard a heavy metal clank.

His head spun as he looked for a hiding place. The people on the other side of the door used the ripper to pull the metal from the frame, sending the bulk metal crashing to the ground and shaking the apartment. One of the black-and-white birds darted away from the explosion and rocketed toward Moss, who couldn't move quickly enough before realizing it was just a hologram.

Or so he thought. The little tit slammed into Moss's chest, falling to the ground and twitching before becoming still. Moss let out a short breath, wondering what this little bird's life had been like. Short and sad. It had probably never left this small space. Never taken a breath outside these walls.

His eyes turned toward the front of the apartment. Moss understood that whoever was breaking in wasn't messing around. He had to find out who they were. Looking at the bedroll, he knew he should hide. Duck away and survive. But he had come too far, done too much and lost too many to sit back. He pulled his Kingfisher and pressed his body next to the door, looking through the room where Issy was hiding and out into the smoking main room.

Through the dust and debris walked three figures. Moss couldn't tell if they were man or machine. Or, likely, a bit of both. They were the shape of humans and too bulky to be pure machine; but there was too much machinery to be the usual cybernetic exoskeleton. They were unique, not quite like anything Moss had ever seen. Their faces were digital plates, scanning and flashing red symbols. He wondered if it was another non-verbal communication but one that couldn't be hacked like neural comms.

Moss, get back, Seti warned and he watched as the figures seemed to have intercepted the communication. He couldn't stop himself. Raising his gun, he blasted several lethal bolts from his Kingfisher into the lead figure. The other two flashed symbols at one another and ducked for cover. Issy burst out, shooting Moss a curious look.

"Right," she said and Moss nodded. He moved through the room and out into the open space. The light of false day shone down, making it hard to see. Bullets fired from behind an abandoned cart full of rice bags. Moss leapt out of the way as Issy rolled right, her weapon trained at some wooden rice barrels. The bullets struck one of the screens, its serene scene immediately turning into a flashing error message.

As soon as one invader poked the top of its head out from behind a barrel, Issy put a bullet through it. She was good. She had always been good. In video games as kids and in real life. Moss had depended too much on his instinct but Issy was the perfect combination of instinct and trained skill.

Moss had his weapon trained at the cart, waiting for the last man-machine to show himself. No dice. Moss kept having to move forward, flipping his pistol to stun. They needed answers.

"Drop the weapon and come out with your hands up," Issy commanded.

"Fuck off, anarchists," a voice rasped with a digital overlay.

"That's a new one," Moss said to Issy as the two moved to close in on the figure.

"Right," Issy said and strafed to get a better angle. The cart was against the wall, so the figure was covered on two sides; but it was low so they had it cornered. "We get terrorist a lot, but anarchist is a new one."

Moss let his eyes dart to Issy and she caught the look. In a flash, she sprang forward, rolling behind the cart with her weapon drawn. The figure couldn't help but turn to watch the blur, taking a few shots that crashed into the dirt. Moss seized the opportunity to fire one blue bolt into the back of the attacker. Its body went rigid and both he and Issy were on it in a flash. Moss moved and pulled its hands back, closing them together with cable ties.

Issy moved in like a striking snake, her weapon at the ready. Reaching out, she began to pull at the base of the helmet.

"Dumb fucks," the voice said, but Issy pulled her hand back before the electric shock its suit released could get her.

"Not as dumb as you," she said and pressed her weapon against its temple.

"Who do you work for?" Moss asked.

The laugh that crackled out of the head sent a chill down Moss's spine. "You don't even know who you are fighting?" It laughed in pure delight. "You have to be the dumbest fuckers in the world. We will take down your organization in no time."

"Big talk from a ... whatever you are in your position," Issy said. Then it clicked.

"He's stal-" Moss blurted but it was too late. He felt his body being blasted forward as the wall burst open behind him. Sizzling metal, bits of debris and earth sprayed through the room. The walls around them began to explode as the hovering vehicle outside assaulted the room with bullets.

As they both ran toward the door, Moss felt a bullet crash through his right leg. The cybernetics sent pain to let the user know they had been hurt but not in the same way the body did. The machinery still functioned, but not as well and his body rocked as he ran.

Going to have them intercepted, jammed my systems, Seti told them in their minds as they ran. Moss saw a mist of blood spray from Issy as she passed through the door into the hallway and crashed to the ground.

"We have to keep moving," Moss said, reaching down to help her up. She was clutching her side and a fear ran through him like he had never experienced before. He had never wanted any of his friends to die, had felt the pain of their loss as if they had been his own family; but seeing Issy hurt was different. He would do anything to keep her safe.

He heard more footfalls crashing toward them.

"Come on," he said.

"I don't think it's that bad," she said, and that made him even more terrified. She always downplayed injuries. When they were kids, she would finish an entire dodgeball game before informing the company teacher that she was pretty sure she had dislocated her shoulder trying to catch a ball.

Helping her up, he moved her in front of him in the narrow hall, putting his body between himself and the elevators and the apartment. He knew she would never have allowed him to do this under normal circumstances, but she was hurt. She kept walking, lurching forward. He could see the blood dripping from between her fingers. Emotions tore at him. He wanted to help her but didn't know that he could.

Then he heard shouting. Looking down the hall, he saw more of the figures rushing toward them. The hall was so long that they were still only small shapes but they were coming up fast. Moss fired a few shots that diffused in the air before getting anywhere near the approaching figures. ·

In here, Moss heard in his mind as an apartment door opened beside them and Issy nearly collapsed inside. It was a dump. Wires covered the floors and fluids streaked the walls. Moss helped Issy to her feet as the door closed behind them. *To the balcony.*

Draping an arm over Moss's shoulder, Issy forced her feet to help just a little as he carried her through the space. People lay around on couches with their heads jacked into power sources, bodies dying while their minds enjoyed a better life. The door to the balcony was little more than a filth-sheened screen. Moss kicked through it.

Stepping out into the rain, he looked around. There was another of these massive buildings across a small street and looking side to side there were endless balconies. Every one was personalized in some small way to differentiate its owners in a sea of carbon copies.

The cab dropped down from the sky and stopped in front of them, the animatronic head turning, the jaw dropping as it said something lost in the rain. The car door opened as Moss turned to see the apartment door begin to constrict unnaturally.

"Come on," he told Issy frantically as he helped her over to the ledge. With wild eyes, she began to climb up on the crumbling concrete wall. Moss held a hand on her back to steady her as she climbed. Suddenly the apartment door was crushed and pulled free. Through the rain and dust inside the apartment, Moss began to fire.

The cloud flashed yellow as the attackers shot back. Moss felt a searing pain in his shoulder as the sound of bullets striking concrete and metal echoed all around him. Issy pulled herself into the cab and Moss turned, stepping up onto the lip. He fired a few more shots toward the figures and began to pull himself into the cab.

Then he heard it.

A single bullet that hit something serious. The cab banked, and Moss let his grip go but it was too late.

He felt himself falling.

CHAPTER 5

His body plummeted toward the earth.

He had been thinking about falling a lot. He had wondered what his grandmother's last moments must have been like. Now he knew. He would know in the exact way that she had — right before dying.

Then he felt the impact. He was hit from the side and his body was enveloped, encased in some quick-drying foam. His body stopped short. It would have broken his neck if not for the case. He couldn't see and the protection smelled like plastic.

He felt his body being lowered and heard muffled sounds as a machine cracked the outside of the casing like a meringue. A piece was peeled back and he gasped, sucking in air and bits of the foam. A drone with flashing orange lights on top blared at him, "Suicide is in violation of the RENTec Building Associates renters' agreement. Use of our rescue services will be billed to you directly." The drone flashed a light and a display screen on the front showed Moss's bleary, wet face before buzzing away.

The breakers always had programs running to scrape their faces from the shared corporate databases so the drone pic wouldn't do anything, but it felt sloppy. Moss struggled to break free, squirming until his body was out of the casing. Chunks of gray fell onto the street as Moss lifted a sore arm to look up at the hovering cab. He stood uneasily. Though he was safe, all the things that had just happened to his body certainly had an effect.

But it didn't matter. Issy was all that mattered. As the cab dropped lower, he saw her slumped against the seat, clutching her side. Jumping in, he saw that coordinates had already been set.

"Hey, Is, look at me," he soothed, sliding in beside her and already feeling the tears well. He could not lose her. She was the only one he couldn't lose. He had seen what too much pain had done to his grandmother; that could not happen to him. He wanted to be an instrument for change, not a weapon of vengeance.

He felt a slam and his vision went white. It was as though he had been punched in the head, but looking around after blinking himself back to reality, there was nothing that could have caused it. He looked down at Issy. Her eyes were vacant but at least they were still open.

"Issy," he said, his heart feeling like it was being pulled from his body. "I love you. You have to stay with me now. I want to marry you, I want to have your babies, or your mine, or you know, you know what I mean," he sobbed, pulling her close, her arm falling loose.

"You have arrived at your destination," the automaton said, the door opening once more. They were in a part of the city Moss didn't recognize and the rain was falling harder now. He picked up Issy and carried her toward the glowing white light with a red cross. The Quix Fix 24-hour Urgent Care was empty as Moss pushed his way in. Two drudges hurried over, beginning scans as they took Issy from Moss's arms.

"Please," he said, as though the machines would work differently because of his pleas.

"Please step over to billing so we may commence treatment," one of the drudges announced as they carried her through some doors. Moss turned to a young person sitting inside a booth beside the door. He had to step over a little bot that was making its way to clean and sanitize the floor of Issy's blood.

"Currency ID number," she asked, looking Moss right in the eyes. Most of the people doing jobs like this were lazy or tired or distracted, but this young woman actually seemed to be taking her job seriously. She wasn't watching some show on a palmscreen or checking her socials on a lenscreen or chatting neurally. She seemed totally present. It surprised Moss that it surprised him so much to see it, though the thought flitted away in a moment as he figured out his next move.

Seti rattled off a clean number that he could use and after he told the girl, she looked at his side. "You could probably go in too?"

He looked down and saw that he was bleeding. His leg was still busted and he didn't know how many other injuries he had. There were bits of the foam in his hair and chunks of wall in the folds of his jacket. He couldn't help but wonder what this young woman saw when she looked at him.

Shaking his head, he stepped over to the vending machine, looking at the digital display and selecting the spray he needed. After payment, it clanked down and he lifted his shirt, coating the long, bloody wound in the fine mist and letting the spray do its work. His leg dragging, he moved back over to the girl who had been watching him the whole time. Her hair was jet black and cut into a bob with bangs across the front.

Smiling, she asked, "Something else I can do for you?"

"Can I go back and see her?" he asked. Now that he had sorted himself out, all he cared about was Issy.

"Ooh," she said, pulling her mouth across gritted teeth. "Actually, the paperwork you just signed expressly forbids visitors."

"I just signed away my own right to see her?" Moss asked, feeling his blood boil.

"I'm so sorry, sir," she said, sounding genuinely sad to report the news — although she had undoubtedly reported it many, many times before to many, many people. "It's company policy."

Moss shook his head.

"But we will send alerts to the number associated with your payment," she informed him.

And I'll be sure to pass them along to you, Seti informed him.

"Fine, okay," Moss said gruffly. "As long as she is being cared for."

"She is," the girl behind the counter said, looking down at her screen. "Appears that she has been stabilized and is being prepped for surgery."

"Okay," Moss said, turning to leave.

"Oh, sir," the girl called after him.

"Yeah?" he asked over a shoulder.

"Can I interest you in a lollipop?"

Moss couldn't help but laugh at the absurdity of it. "Sure," he said and held up a hand, catching the candy with ease. As he stepped out into the rain, he looked at the branding on the pop. It had the name of the clinic and the location, as though a person would forget where they had left their loved one.

Thinking about Issy being there and not being able to help or even see her, he let out a pained bellow. He screamed out all the suffering. He let all the hurt he had known for so long shriek out of his body and into the dark rain. Tears streaked his face, lost in the downpour.

Feel better? Seti asked in his mind once he had finished.

Yes. Ish.

Good, she said. *Get anything we can use?*

Yes, he told her, pulling out the chip and looking at it. *Know any forensic accountants?*

I can do you one better, Seti said and Moss felt as if he could hear the smirk.

"You look like a bag of shit," Judy said, approaching Moss sitting in front of a restaurant.

Looking up from his pork bun, he said, "I feel like a bag of shit."

Judy chuckled and nodded. "Where's Issy?"

"Shot," Moss said and Judy laughed for just a moment before seeing his face and realizing the truth in his words.

They rushed over to join him on the little bench. "Is she okay?"

"I mean, she was shot," Moss said with a shrug. He was ready to move the investigation forward, to find the people who had hurt their allies and Issy, but he also felt that part of himself was back in the urgent care facility.

Judy draped a tattooed arm over Moss. "She's in good hands," they said. "She's tough as shit. Maybe even tougher than Ynna. She just doesn't feel the need to bring it up every other sentence."

Moss chuckled. "Yeah."

"Got your head in the game?" they asked.

Moss nodded, stuck the last bite of food in his mouth and said through stuffed cheeks, "Let's go."

He followed Judy as they made their way up Stockton Street. Moss's mother had tried to teach him some Mandarin when he was a kid, but he didn't remember any of it and couldn't make out any of the signs, posters or neon lights. The words being spoken were as foreign to him as any other language. An old man shuffled past them to flick a cigarette butt at a middle-aged man offloading a pallet of fish before screaming something at him.

There were shops and laundries and cafés lining the street on both sides, all with side doors leading to apartments. They stepped into a restaurant so small that it was little more than a countertop with two plastic tables set in front. One was occupied by what looked to be old friends catching up at one and friends of Bill at the other. Judy walked up to the counter where a little old lady had her back to the counter as she rinsed a dish in a small sink against the back wall.

Judy cleared their throat. The old woman turned, her eyes lighting up when she saw Judy. "Judy, is that you?" she said, smiling and showing crooked yellow teeth.

"It's me, Mei," Judy said, flipping up the board that bisected the counter and stepping back. The woman shuffled over in well-worn fuzzy pink slippers and embraced Judy who was dressed in far less flair than normal. They wore black jeans with a white tank top and black vest.

They hugged a long time and Moss had a guess who this might be.

"How have you been?" the old woman asked.

"Good, Auntie. Given everything."

Mei pulled away but kept her hands on Judy's arms. "You look skinny. Too skinny. And sad. You can't lie to me."

Judy chuckled. "I know it."

"Tell me how you have been."

Judy shook their head. "Bad. Miserable. I miss him every day. Every moment of every day." They gestured to the cracked frame displaying the digital article about the debut of Miners FC striker Stanley Wu.

"Me too," Mei said. "But he loved you," she said sweetly, her voice full of joyful reminiscence. "He loved you more than I have ever seen love."

"I know," Judy said, their voice breaking. Mei wrapped them up once again and Judy let out a low wail. It had been so long since Stan had been killed and so much had happened since then. But for Judy, this loss would be the one that lasted forever.

They cried together a long time. Mei finally wiped away a tear and said, "I know you are not here for my shitty dumplings."

"The dumplings aren't shitty," one of the patrons called out.

"Oh, shut up, Dennis," Mei called to him, waving a hand. "You think after fifty years, one compliment is going to get you into my apron?"

"Worth a shot," Dennis said and Moss saw a small smile cross Judy's lips.

"We are here to see Charles," Judy told Mei.

The old woman shook her head. "That's what I was worried about."

"I know he doesn't want to see me," Judy said. "I know he blames me ... for everything."

Mei nodded. "You bring a peace offering?"

"I did," Judy said.

Mei moved out of the way after punching in a code beside the door behind the counter. The door swung open, leading to little more than a tight staircase. It reminded Moss of the apartment hallway and of Issy, but he knew he couldn't

51

dwell. Judy began to ascend, but the old woman grabbed Moss's wrist.

"You affected him more than you'll ever know," she said, winking before letting his arm go.

"Thank you," he cracked and followed Judy up the stairs to a small landing with another blank door. This one was heavy metal with nothing more than a horizontal slot at the front. It slid open.

"No!" a man's voice said from behind the door and the rectangle closed.

"Charles," Judy pleaded.

"No," came muffled through the door. "I already told Seti we didn't have anything to do with it."

Moss connected the dots. "We need your help with something else," he offered. "We'll pay."

Judy pulled out a liquor bottle with a Chinese label Moss didn't recognize and held it up just before the little door slid open again.

"Fuck is this?" said the voice that Moss presumed to be Charles's. "Think one bottle of nice booze is enough to make up for what you did?"

"It's more than just one bottle," Judy said. "I got you a deal for cases of this shit for a pittance. Let me in and you can flood the streets with it."

The little door slid closed again and Moss heard voices speaking to one another. Then the door itself opened and a man in his late thirties appeared. He wore a grey tank top, fashionable ripped pants and tattoos on every visible patch of skin.

"What you need?" he asked abruptly.

The room behind him was quite a sight, the opposite of the apartment they had just visited. Dingy, grimy and unkempt, it was littered with cigarette butts coating the stained red carpet, ancient, yellowed newspaper coating the windows and white plastic tables all around the room. One was covered in a pile of weapons, another in handbags, one in cybernetics and the last in a pile of powder. A naked woman in a collar sat at a computer in the corner and two beefy men sat on a couch, watching soccer and stoking their guns in a blatant show of force.

"First," Judy said, "I need to tell you how sorry I am for your loss."

The man's face pulled into a tight mask. It was obvious he was Stan's brother. They had nearly identical faces, although this man's was harder, more worn with age and toughness. Stan had been a brawler and a beast but this man seemed weathered by a hard life. Charles was not quite as large as his brother; Stan had been a giant man, tall from birth but muscled from years of workouts. The gangster brother was no slouch, though, and looked as if he had been in a fight every day of his adult life. His body was toned and inked skin hard. He had no cybernetics.

"First," he said, stepping forward, fists clenched, "I don't give a fuck that you're sorry."

Judy smirked. Their fists balled as well. "I'm sorry regardless of whether you give a fuck."

"Your crusade got him killed," Charles said, pointing a finger and getting in Judy's face. The two men on the couch turned their attention to the scene unfolding. The younger of the two, a skinny kid with floppy black hair, seemed nervous. Moss knew he had to be ready for a fight. He was exhausted and beaten, but he could pull a pistol if needed.

Judy didn't back down. "Oh, bullshit! Yes, he got killed running a job for us, but do you think he would have lasted doing what you wanted him to? Your shit nearly got him killed long before mine."

"Nearly," Charles hissed.

They looked poised to throw down. Moss felt his hand shift slightly toward his weapon. It was draining to feel like he was going to battle for his life every minute of the day.

"You know how much this has fucked me up?" Judy said, taking a different tactic. "Your brother wasn't just a cash cow for me, wasn't just something I could use to rig matches. He was the love of my life."

Charles bolted forward to loom over them. "He was my brother!"

They stared at one another a long time and then he wrapped his arms around them.

"I am sorry for your loss too," he whispered. Neither wept though both seemed to want to. "What is it that I can do for you?"

CHAPTER 6

"We need you to tell us who loaded this chip," Judy told him.

Charles's lip turned up. "What'd they do?"

"None of your business," Judy said with a sad smile. Moss could tell they had a complicated history but was happy that their mutual love of Stan had brought them together. The man had died what felt like so long ago and yet he was still having a positive impact.

"Let me see the chip," Charles said, extending a hand. Judy shook their head and gestured to Moss, who fished the thing out of his pocket. Charles plucked it up and walked it over to the naked girl. Scars crisscrossed her back. He said something to her in Chinese.

"How much for her?" Moss couldn't help but ask. He hated to see it. He knew he was dealing with gangs and that they did nasty shit all the time but being faced with it was something else. He thought about Jitters and all she had suffered to help people just like this girl. He thought about Zip Thud, the young man who died for hacking into a smuggling ring's computer network.

"She's not for sale," Charles said flatly. Part of Moss wished he could just offload his weapon into the men in this room. It didn't matter that it was Stan's brother or that they had an entire gang at their backs. Moss was angry and hated to see the girl in chains, hated that Issy had been hurt and their allies were being killed. He had so much anger and no place to put it. Well, not yet anyway.

"Human or relief aide?" Moss asked through gritted teeth.

"Would it matter?" he said with a grin. "Programmed feelings hurt just the same."

The comment sent a chill down Moss's spine as he thought about the implications.

Judy put a hand on Moss's shoulder to calm him and he took a deep breath. Seeing a pack of Chunghwas on the table, he walked over and pulled one out, lighting it with the Bic beside it. It was the perfect distraction from everything.

The girl looked up at Charles, terror in her eyes, and spoke. He nodded and walked over to them. "She says it was loaded by Rigg Fingers," he explained and gave them the address.

Moss sighed. "Thank you," he said, happy to have a direction to go, a lead to follow. The gangster nodded and exchanged a look with Judy before Judy joined Moss in the hallway.

Plus, you have a meeting later, Seti introjected. *With our contact at D2E.*

"No rest for the weary," Judy said.

"Mind joining me?" Moss asked. He didn't want to be alone with his thoughts or with a mind that seemed to be breaking.

Judy smiled. "Try and stop me."

"Thanks," Moss said. Then he asked, *Seti, any word on Issy?*

I'll tell you as soon as I hear, she told him, and Judy clapped him on the back reassuringly.

They stepped through the restaurant once more and Mei handed them a plastic bag that smelled delectable.

"Thank you, Auntie," Judy said.

"Don't let it be so long," she said with a friendly smile that creased her face. "I'm happy you didn't come to blows," she added.

Judy huffed and smiled. "Me too."

As they walked down the street, Judy said, "You know we can't save everyone."

"I know," Moss said. "I just hate to see that shit."

"Maybe it was an android." Judy shrugged.

"And if not?"

"If not," they said, contemplating the words as they pushed through morning crowd, "then it's part of the fucked-up shit we aim to fix."

"He looks just like him, sorta," Moss observed.

Judy nodded. "Couldn't be more different."

"No kidding," Moss remarked as they continued down the street. "He really blamed you?"

Judy let out a long, thoughtful sigh. "No, I don't think he ever actually did. I think he blamed himself for a lot of things and pointed his anger at me because it was easier. I know he and the rest of his family were upset that we couldn't honor the body … that still sits with me, too."

They trailed off and Moss felt a pang of guilt. He had left Carcer City wounded and captured, but it still hurt that he couldn't give his friend the sendoff he deserved.

Moss tried to choke down his emotions as they turned the corner and saw the cab still hovering nearby. There were bloodstains and bullet holes and the side was smoking, yet Moss couldn't help but chuckle at the sight of it in the golden morning sun.

"Riding in style," Moss said as they both climbed in.

"Right," Judy said. "At least we won't draw any attention in this or anything …"

"We are here," Judy said, nudging Moss awake as the cab lowered.

"Where are we?" he asked, looking around and seeing more grey buildings with more neon lights.

Judy laughed at the question. "You know, some other part of this fucking sprawl," they said. "Just around the corner from Rigg Fingers."

Moss rubbed his face, the sweat and natural grease making it easy. "Just when I think the names these people have can't get any stupider."

"I'm sure it means something to them." Judy held out a hand to help Moss down. His side was starting to hurt again. "Also, Seti said Issy is out of surgery and stable. No vital organs. She'll be up and running in no time."

"Can we . . ." he said and stopped, shaking his head.

"We have things to do."

"No, right, I know."

They started down the street. It appeared to be nearly noon and Moss wondered what part of the city this was. The weather was warm enough and enough time had passed that he knew they were nowhere near downtown anymore. Moss pulled his jacket off and sucked in the hot air.

The buildings here were shorter and fatter than those downtown and the people were all dressed in shorts and tank tops and had tans. It seemed strange but Moss realized he didn't leave the heart of the city all that often.

"Want to stop here?" Judy asked, pointing at a Teotl Coffee.

Moss nodded, and soon they were making their way down the street with coffees in hand.

"We look like partners in a crime drama," Moss noted.

Judy laughed. "You know Carcer paid D2E to make most of those shows. It was good PR for them. It made it seem like the company was out to help the average person rather than oppress him."

Judy pointed to a brick apartment complex down the street.

"You know what's fun?" Moss asked ironically.

"What's that?"

"Learning that literally everything you have ever enjoyed is part of some massive corporate ploy to control you," he said, face flat. "Since I have left the burb, that has been my whole life. There is nothing left anymore that I can enjoy without knowing there is some scumbag somewhere profiting off it or some little guy somewhere suffering because of it."

"I suppose I am sorry that is the nature of the world," Judy offered, reaching over and breaking off a piece of Moss's vanilla frosted donut. "Does it help to know that we are going to get information that can help us stop people from hurting our allies and then meet with someone else who can expose your former employer for being a dastardly villain?"

"It helps that you used the term 'dastardly villain,' honestly," Moss said with a weak smile.

"I thought it might."

Judy grinned briefly as they approached the steps to the building, wide with faded bricks. The lower apartments had metal bars over the windows and a bank of mailboxes built into the little foyer at the front.

"Guess it would have been too easy to have a mailbox with the name Fingers on it?" Moss said as he appraised the list.

Judy dropped their faded green backpack to the ground and began rummaging, pulling out a small drone they cast into the air while donning digital display glasses.

"What are you looking for?" Moss asked.

"Nothing."

Moss grumbled and shook his head. "I suppose I can just go fuck myself."

"The fucking theatrics," Judy scoffed. "Nothing is what I am looking for. Most normal people's apartments will have normal electrical output and wiring. If Rigg is into shady business, he will probably have a graymaker running. Like this," they said as if Moss could see in the glasses. They craned their neck and pointed up to the corner of the building. "Two, probably A," they said.

Moss nodded, selecting an apartment number at random and pressing the call button. A voice answered after a moment. "Hello?"

"Delivery," Moss said and the door to the building instantly buzzed open. "People are so fucking dumb," he observed.

"Real nice. Not that it's untrue, I just don't expect it from you."

"My girlfriend's in urgent care," Moss snapped. "You'll have to forgive me for not being my normal, chipper self."

Judy smiled sadly as they began to walk up to the apartment. "Now you can perhaps understand why I needed some time to myself a bit ago."

Moss shook his head. "We told you we understood."

"Still, it's nice to hear it again sometimes."

On the second floor, they turned left and walked to the end of the hall. Moss tried to communicate with Seti to hack the door as they approached but the dampener was strong enough to prevent it. As they stepped up, they looked with surprise at the door. It was rotted wood, not the reinforced metal they had been expecting.

Judy pulled traditional lockpicks out of their pocket and knelt to use them, but when they were about to begin, Moss put a hand on their shoulder. "This is someone who works with people who support us," he whispered, not sure if there was a person looking at them from the door opposite. "How about we just knock."

"Guess that's an option too," Judy said, putting away the lockpicks and pulling out a large revolver.

Moss shook his head and began to knock, but when his fist contacted the door, it swung open. "That's never a good sign," he said.

Judy simply said, "Fuck."

They pushed the door open with the muzzle of their weapon and the stink hit them first. They saw nothing noteworthy as they walked in, but something had happened here. The door opened into a living room with a large display screen, a couch and a biocase for extended VR time. All the curtains were drawn and Judy hit a switch on the wall to open them. Light filled the room but there was still nothing.

"You go right," they said and Moss shook his head.

"Splitting up is a sure-fire way to get us both killed," he observed quietly.

Judy just shook their head and began walking down a small hallway, following the bundled cords taped to the ceiling. There were no pictures on the wall or anything that made the apartment feel like a home. Moss wondered if Rigg moved often for security.

"Oh, shit." Judy gagged as they rounded a corner and Moss's eyes went wide as he saw it. The curtains were slowly rising in the bedroom, allowing a slow reveal of the scene. Blood was everywhere. Chunks of body and slices of skin, parts of fingers and pieces of scalp were strewn about.

Written in blood on the wall were the words, "Death to anarchists."

CHAPTER 7

"What is going on here?" Moss nearly spat. "Who are these people and what is their fucking problem?"

"Former Carcer? ThutoCo?" Judy asked.

"That seems like the best guess," Moss said, staring at the viscera all around them. "But why do all this?"

"Is it too on-the-nose to say, 'to send a message?'" Judy said, eyes scanning the room.

"You're right, but this is really fucked."

He tried to look past all the blood and gore to the room, the scene. If they wanted information, they needed to get a sense of what happened here. Judy's small drone began scanning, taking in all the room's data. The recreation it would be able to project later would have so much more information than just looking at it would provide.

But Moss felt that there was something to be said for actually being in the place. He followed the bundled cables out of the bedroom and into a small, dark room through a door that could be padlocked from the inside.

The room was small with little more than a computer setup and chair. There was some machinery in the room too, but as with everything else it had been destroyed. Whoever had been here had been thorough.

Moss wished they had captured one of the attackers back at the ancient Japan apartment, that things had gone differently and they had gotten some answers rather than another dead end. He groaned, picking up a piece of what looked like motherboard and tossing it on the pile. This man, whoever Rigg Fingers had been, had died for their cause. Moss had known so much personal loss but he never stopped to think about all the others he didn't know who had died as well.

"I'm sorry, Rigg," he said.

Moss heard a noise and nearly jumped out of his skin. His weapon was drawn in an instant and trained in no particular direction. He heard it again, like a little rattle coming from inside the walls. A rat, he supposed. But looking down, he saw an open vent, just large enough for a child to crawl into. His heart sank. Kids growing up in this city saw some grim stuff, but this would mess a person up forever. He knelt, moving aside some more metal scraps.

Peering into the dark, he squinted at the vent.

"Hello," he said in as kind a voice as he could muster. "I am not here to hurt you."

He heard a vague noise but no reaction — no breathing or shifting.

"I am a friend of Rigg's," Moss offered. "If you come on out, I will help you."

Still nothing.

"Moss?" Judy called from somewhere else in the apartment. "You talking to me?"

Moss ignored them. "That's my friend, Judy," he said into the dark, his voice now light and sweet. "I would love to introduce you to them. Why don't you come on out and we can help you. The bad people are gone."

He heard movement.

After a moment, a small sphere the size of a soccer ball rolled out. A digital cutesy robot face was displayed at the front, which remained in place even as it moved. The eyes were big and scared and the mouth pinched closed.

Moss opened his arms, beckoning it forward. "Hey, kiddo," he said warmly.

Then he jolted.

He caught himself, hands down in a pile of scrap metal, but his body had been forced down as though he had been punched in the temple.

The little ball robot retreated at the movement and Moss gasped out a breath to steady himself, grateful that he had already been kneeling.

"It's okay," Moss assured the robot, though he was also trying to convince himself.

"You are my ... friend?" the robot asked in a childlike voice.

"Yes," Moss said. "I am a friend."

"The bad men were not my friends," the bot said, its eyes displaying fear. "They hurt my Rigg."

"I know," Moss said. "They hurt my Rigg too," he said, pretty sure Issy would not be thrilled about the comparison.

"Oh," the bot said.

"I'm Moss."

"I'm . . ." he began, but he was interrupted by a recording of an angry voice saying, "Stupid cunting thing making me pick a name . . ." Then it beeped. The ball's voice returned to say, "But I go by Stu."

"It's nice to meet you, Stu," Moss said. "Would you like me to get you out of here."

"Yes, please," Stu said, the automated voice sounding thankful.

Moss held out his hands and it rolled up onto them. "You may want to shut off your sensors for a moment," he warned.

"I will," Stu said, the digital eyes closing. For a moment, the eyes reminded Moss of Zip and the digital plate he had. Or had had.

Groaning as he stood, Moss moved back into the bloodbath and stepped through the room, calling down the hall to Judy.

"In here," they answered and Moss followed the sound of their voice.

As he rounded the corner into the bathroom, his hand shot over what seemed to be the front of the ball. In the bathtub was what Moss had to assume had been Rigg. He was mostly whole but had fingers removed and slices of skin cut off. Moss couldn't look at it and jumped back out of the room. Stu made a horrified squeak and tried to roll. Moss held him tightly and spoke in a soothing voice, "It's okay, it's going to be okay."

"No! No! No!" Stu wailed and kept trying to move. Moss would not let go. He thought that if he lost the bot now, he would never get him back. Pressing hard against the movement, he continued to try and reassure the bot.

Judy stepped out. Moss wasted no time. "This is our friend, Stu."

"Hi, Stu," Judy said kindly.

The bot stopped trying to spin. "They hurt my friend," it cried.

"I know," Judy said. "But we are here to help you and protect you from those bad men."

"Oh, okay," the bot said. "If you are friends of Rigg, you are a friend of Stu."

Judy shot Moss a look and he shrugged.

"Can you tell us what happened here?" Judy asked, tucking their zebra-dyed hair behind an ear.

"Rigg had made himself a supper of Suggi-O's in the microwave. He prepared it in his favorite ceramic bowl that has an image of the Hapi Napples at the bottom. That way, when you finish, you —"

Judy held up a hand.

"Can we skip to the part where the bad men came?"

A dejected face flashed on Stu and Moss shot Judy a look.

"As we finished the episode of Tink Tink Revolution, Nove was eliminated even though Dexter had a much worse performance. Rigg said that he thought it was because the producers —"

Judy's face tightened and they sighed before saying, "Then there was a knock at the door?"

"Yes," Stu said. Moss adjusted the ball so it was easier for them both to see it. "But the knock was not the traditional three knocks lightly. It was six knocks hard. It seemed as if the person was using the base of a fist instead of the expected knuckles. Rigg suggested that the difference in knocking style was to send a message. I asked what kind of message and he said —"

This time, Moss cut it off. "Did Rigg answer the door?"

"No, he got up and ERROR," Stu shrieked and Judy covered their ears. Moss nearly dropped the ball. "Information lock. Please see the manufacturer for more details."

"Fuck!" Judy said. "Guessing the company does not want their units describing extreme violence."

Moss closed his eyes and tried to calm himself. "Every. Time. We. Get. Close."

"Well, hey there, little guy," Patchwork said as Stu rolled into the kitchen.

"Hey there, big guy," Stu said. Patch smiled. He was dressed in fashionable sweatpants and had his hair pulled back and bundled with a loose piece of cabling tied together. As he always did, he wore a tee shirt with some niche anime character on the front. He and Gibbs had bonded over their mutual love of representing the media they enjoyed.

Another young man stepped out of Patchwork's room, dressed as though he were ready for combat. His clothes were all dark and had pockets, zippers and hooks filled with everything a person could need in an emergency. His head was shaved and his face severe, but he smiled when he saw Stu and then looked shocked to see Moss.

"Oh, hello," he said and then cleared his throat to deepen his voice and said, "Hello, sir."

Patchwork's whole face brightened and he turned as if in slow motion. "What the fuck was that?"

"Nothing, shut up," the young man said out of the corner of his mouth.

Moss cocked his head, feeling like he had seen the militaristic kid before and not in the context of him coming out of Patchwork's room. "I know you?"

"Yes, sir," he said. "I mean, we don't know one another, that is to say we have never met, but we do know each other in the professional sense."

Moss looked at Patchwork. "I don't feel any more informed."

Patch simply beamed and said, "Oh, I'm gonna let him do this on his own. It's amazing to watch."

The young man let his shoulders drop and sighed. "Ugh, fine, I've made enough of an ass of myself," he said and turned to Moss. Even deflated, he was large and muscular. "I'm Tak. I've made a name for myself setting up safehouses for us and I just got my own crew recently."

"Oh! That's how I know you," Moss said, smiling up at him. "By reputation, but a good reputation."

"Thank you," Tak said with a huge smile. "Thank you, sir!"

Moss shook his head. "I am not into that 'sir' stuff.".

"Not what Issy said," Judy said from over his shoulder and Patchwork burst out laughing.

"I was *just* about to say that!" he squealed in delight.

Moss shook his head and muttered, "Assholes."

Tak looked at Patch with horrified astonishment. "You speak to him this way?"

Patchwork pushed Tak's shoulder. "He's not a stuck-up, self-made hero guy," Patch said with a smirk. "Moss's parents were amazing badasses and it turns out he kinda is too, but he's still half a bub."

Moss considered the words. "Pretty accurate, really."

Patchwork nodded triumphantly as Tak just stared.

"I could still kick your ass, though." Moss winked at Patch.

"Couldn't kick anything with that broke-ass leg," Patch said.

Judy tapped Moss on the shoulder. "Let's go get that sorted."

Moss nodded and looked down at Stu, whose digital display smiled up at them. "Go with my friend Patchwork and he will help you out."

"Patchwork is less commonly a name and more commonly a noun meaning something made up of an incongruous variety of pieces or parts," Stu said.

Patch nodded as though to a child he was trying to humor. "That's right."

"Is Patchwork your given name?" Stu asked as they began moving through the kitchen.

"No," Patch said. "Stu yours?"

"No," the robot admitted and they disappeared with Tak hot on their heels.

"That new?" Moss asked Judy, nodding at Tak's disappearing form.

They shrugged. "I look like I give a fuck?"

"You are really so unsatisfying to gossip with."

"I look like I give a fuck?"

Moss rolled his eyes. "Fine, let's just fix my fucking leg and meet with this D2E guy."

Judy grabbed a bottle of whisky off the counter and smiled. "Now you're talking my language."

CHAPTER 8

"It hadn't taken long for Judy to get Moss's leg back up and running and it had been nice to take a little break. They drank a bit and chatted about nothing in particular. They both needed it. Moss felt as though he had been able to breathe for the first time in a long time as he spoke about Issy and the future.

"It's the proximity to death," he said, the sweat beading around his head. It wasn't particularly hot in Judy's workshop but the drink had taken effect.

"*That*, I can understand," they said solemnly.

Moss looked up at Judy, studying their face. They were attractive and still young. The light makeup they wore always accentuated their features just right and the zebra-striped hair was just so cool.

"Do you think . . ." he began but trailed off.

They waited, now studying his face.

"You think you'll ever date again?"

The most miserable smile Moss had ever seen crossed their lips, and they let out a little laugh. "No," they said. "I can't imagine it. I'll fuck again, but I can't see being intimate again."

"Why?" Moss said, though he felt he knew the answer. All of them shared the one answer. They had all lost so many people who were close to them and that damage ran deep.

"Feel like I used up all my points," they said, staring down into their drink.

Moss furrowed his brows. That was not the answer he was expecting. He didn't speak; he just stared until they continued.

"After everything with my family on the Big Island, I felt I only had a finite amount of heart left. As if there was only so much in the reserve. When I met Stan, he got it all, or almost all, anyway." They trailed off. Moss put a hand on theirs. He knew what Judy was trying to say.

"I have to ask you something," they said, looking over at him and absentmindedly clicking a sparker.

"Shoot," Moss said as he pulled on the front of his shirt repeatedly to blow air on his face.

"You haven't really talked about what happened that night," they said and Moss knew what they were getting at. "The wedding night."

Moss fell out of his chair. Or rather, he collapsed to the ground as though he had been slapped upside the head. Hitting the concrete, he sputtered and coughed. Judy rushed to his side.

"What the fuck was that?" they exclaimed, hopping down from the amp they had been sitting on to help Moss to his feet.

"I don't really know," he admitted.

"Is it the program?" Judy asked, their face a mask of worry.

Moss nodded. "I think so."

"We have to tell Patchwork," they insisted, making for the door.

Moss grabbed their elbow and shook his head, saying, "He needs to focus on Stu and getting the information on who killed his owner. That's what's important for the cause."

Judy laughed at him. "*You* are what is important for the cause. Did you see the way that kid reacted to you? Do you realize the scope of the missions we have run? The fact that you helped kill Warden Ninety-Nine and cripple Carcer?

"You may not appreciate your role in the world now.

"You are a figurehead, a beacon, a symbol of everything we are trying to accomplish. The young bub who woke up one day to see the world for what it was and wanted to change it. That's the kind of shit people rally around.

"I know you sometimes feel like you are being carried along or that the rest of us lift you up or that you are just here because of your parents and," they grinned, "while some of that is true, you have also come into your own."

Moss smiled. "Thanks," he said, rubbing his temple.

"All of that isn't to blow smoke up your ass but to make the fucking point that if your program is broken, it needs fixing," Judy snapped and once again made their way toward the door.

Moss moved in front of them. "Look, I know I need to get this all sorted out. But this whole thing has been a problem from the word go and we don't have time to deal with this shit. We need him to keep looking into who is coming after us and you and I need to be ready to meet our contact. If we can't get the word out about ThutoCo, all of this is for nothing. We can keep fighting them, but without the support of the public, the company and their pals on the AIC will get us."

"I know all of this," Judy said impatiently, "but you just got knocked out of your seat by your own brain. That shit takes priority."

"How about I promise to have it looked at as soon as we get back," Moss said. He wasn't sure why he was fighting this so hard. He just didn't want to think about it. With Issy hurt and everything else they had going on, he really didn't want to worry about the program. He was just sick of thinking about the program altogether. It was starting to feel like more trouble than it was worth — a weapon used at a cost too great to justify.

The contact is ready to meet you guys, Seti let them know and Moss grinned from ear to ear.

"Saved by the bell," he said with a smile.

Judy just shook their head. "You shouldn't be so fucking pleased with yourself, Moss," they said solemnly. "This is scary shit and you need to get it sorted as soon as we are done with this."

"I promise," Moss said. Judy's concern was touching. *So*, Moss communicated to Seti, *where we heading?*

You are not going to believe it, Seti told them and Moss felt like he could hear her smirk.

The streets of B.A. City were always crowded. Masses of people moved in throngs pressed shoulder to shoulder.

This was nothing compared to where Moss and Judy found themselves. Every inch of the space seemed to be packed with humans, everyone dressed for the occasion. People wore outfits bearing the D2E brand image, the font or characters from the movies. Almost everyone wore hats or headbands with different versions of Stan the Gopher's famous ears. They carried bags full of more toys than a kid could play with in a lifetime or enough treats to give every tooth a cavity. Rented scooters meant half the patrons didn't have to walk between attractions, many built hundreds of years earlier. Parents screamed at their children to "Have fun!" and the kids whined for a screen they would rather be playing with.

Pushing through the fans had been exhausting since they had arrived at D2Eland to meet the contact. Moss couldn't understand why this location was chosen, but the contact suggested it was the one place they wouldn't be looking, right under their own noses.

Moss and Judy had stopped by a shop on the way and purchased costumes to blend in all the more. Moss wore a shirt and pants reminiscent of the D2E animated Robin Hood and Judy had a shirt with the words "not all princesses are born" written in the twirly font the company was known for.

Moss felt overwhelmed. A band played a song he vaguely recognized from some movie as a world class animatronic pirate posed for pictures with adults trying to recapture their youths. Judy took a bite of the gopher-shaped pretzel and offered it to Moss, who just shook his head as they approached the bench they were told to find. It had only taken about twenty minutes to walk from the front gate to the middle of the Old West portion of the park, but it had felt to Moss like three hours.

He gasped as he sat. Judy plonked down next to him and smiled.

"You like this shit?" he asked incredulously.

They shook their head and laughed. "Lots of kids who grew up in less than ideal circumstances were raised on D2E movies. Long before I knew the truth about these companies, I escaped into their fantasies and saw myself in the characters going on amazing quests and escaping hard lives.

"The people here waiting for hours to ride a rickety boat through a dark room of puppets are reconnecting to the joy that seems to die a little bit with every year we live. All these people could just run into the Mass Illusion, live the movies that made them happy as children, but they would rather experience the shared joy of being here."

Moss's mouth fell open. "I swear, Jude, that was the most romantic thing I think I have ever heard you say … and I watched you officiate a wedding."

Judy chuckled and bumped their shoulder into Moss's. "I'm just saying that I get it."

"Good that one of us does," he snorted. "This whole place just seems like the worst type of corporate-controlled hivemindery ever designed to separate people from their money for shit they don't need."

"You'll never understand what it can mean to someone who needed a connection and found one with one of the movies or saw a better life for themselves," they said in an uncharacteristically wistful tone.

Moss found it hard not to laugh. "You going to stay after the meeting?" he asked sarcastically.

Judy looked at him flatly. "Yes."

"You Che?" a voice said. Moss and Judy turned and Moss nodded, scooting over to allow the man room. He was an older man in jeans and a grey tee shirt. His graying, curly black hair was pulled into a tie and he had a hat pulled low over his face with mirror shades covering his eyes. Moss wanted to laugh at the ridiculously conspicuous outfit.

"Hey, I'm The Contact," he said conspiratorially.

Judy laughed. "You are obviously Rude Von 'Tude," they said and the man looked around as though the world would take note.

"Don't … don't say that name," he said, but once Judy had pointed it out, Moss could tell it was the aging infotainment shock jock.

"You think D2E is watching you that closely?" Judy asked, rolling their eyes.

A scowl crossed the man's face. "No, you imbecile. My fans! If they see me, they will mob me and this will all be for naught."

"We understand," Moss soothed, shooting a sidelong glance at Judy.

"How would you like it if I started shouting Moss all over the place?" the man hissed.

Moss couldn't help but look around. No one cared. Everyone was making their way to or from somewhere and not listening to this conversation.

"I take your point," he said, wishing conversations with allies went as smoothly as some with supposed enemies.

"I'm here to help you, I'll remind you," he said.

Moss let out a slow exhalation, watching as a woman accidentally spilled popcorn into another person's stroller and walked away before they noticed.

"You're right. Thank you," Moss said, turning back to look at him. The man seemed visibly nervous. He was fidgety and rubbing his pant leg between his fingers.

"What can you tell us?" Moss asked.

The man seemed to calm down. "I have worked at D2E a long time... a loooong time, you know? And so, I have seen some shit. Some real shit. Like, I know where the bodies are buried."

He paused for dramatic effect and Moss nodded, understanding that the showman would require constant feedback to get his point out.

"I'll bet," Moss added for good measure.

"Right, I knew you would and you would be right to," he said. "When you have been with one of the companies as long as I have, you understand just how evil they are, just how bad and rotten."

This time, Moss knew to fill the pause. "I was raised by ThutoCo. I know how bad they can get."

Rude laughed. "ThutoCo wishes it was D2E. That's where the real evil resides."

"Sure," Judy said. "But maybe we could stop comparing size and get to the fucking point."

"You got some brass ones on you," Rude said with a laugh at his own witticism.

Moss held out a hand. "Listen, friend, we really appreciate you taking the time to chat with us, but I think it is important that you just get to the meat of it. We really have many pressing matters."

"And I don't?" he asked, offended at the implication. Judy stood and pushed through the crowd toward SteampunkLand.

Moss sighed. He was exhausted by this man. "You want my help taking down the company you work for. What can I do?"

Rude sucked on his teeth. "The thing you have to understand is that it all comes down from the top. The managers all have their own agendas, sure, but it's the big man himself who pulls all the strings. The fish rots from the head, as they say."

"If you are telling me that killing the head of an evil company would solve a problem, this is not news to me," Moss said. He was done flattering the man.

"You really are an impatient little prick, aren't you?" Rude said, appraising Moss over the rim of his glasses.

"Yes," Moss said, "I am."

That made Rude smile, showing the wrinkles that no amount of surgery could hide.

"Good, I am too. So, you may know that taking down Derek Sterling, President of D2E, would be a key to your plans, but what you don't know is that I can get you in a room with him. I can get you in a place where you can chop off that rotting head while I get whatever story you want out on the air."

"*Now* you're talking," Moss said with a smile. "But," he added, unable to help himself, "why set up this whole meeting? Why not just let Seti know to let us know?"

Rude gave Moss a miserable smile and put a hand on his upper back, pressing around the back of his neck and swaying Moss a bit. It made Moss want to move away but he could tell the man was about to speak honestly for the first time.

"I wanted to meet you. I have been working as an undercover agent for so long, I just wanted to look into the eyes of the man who was actually bringing some change to this world.

"I know I'm a prick. Shit, being a prick has made me rich; but I am also a person, you know? I am not just the character I play — although sometimes I feel like I have been playing it for so long that I am not sure how much of the real man is left."

Moss let out a little laugh. "I'm not sure how much of me there really was to begin with."

Rude nodded, looking out into the sea of people. "That why you do this? To find yourself?"

Moss blinked hard, considering the question. He had not taken much time to think about why he was doing this. The loss was the obvious answer. ThutoCo had robbed him of his family, of his childhood. The other megas had killed his friends and tried to hack his brain. But was that why he did it? He shook his head.

"It's complicated."

"It always is." Rude nodded.

"How about you?"

"Not so complicated. I started out as an intern at the station. Learned pretty quick that it was easy to get people's attention with shitty stunts but also that a society so numb was hard to shock anymore.

"I got famous for putting a shock collar on a couple of Old Faith hotties and making them run around the city, taking their clothes off or getting electrocuted. Took off and I built a career out of it. Soon, though, I got sick of what I was doing. Looking at myself in the mirror made me want to vomit. I couldn't stand that I was hurting people so that other people would love me. I wanted out. I needed out..." he trailed off.

"They wouldn't let you," Moss filled in and Rude slowly tapped his finger to his nose.

"As you would expect, there is much more sob to my story but you get the picture," he said.

"I do," Moss said. "Well, you get me a meeting and I'll get you out of there."

"Thanks," Rude said wearily. "I always say that not all folks from the burbs are bubs.

CHAPTER 9

"Fucking prick!" Judy seethed and took a step forward.

"Yeah," Moss agreed, "but he lightened up after you left."

"Of course he fucking did," they hissed.

The woman in front of them covered her son's ears and stared daggers back at them.

"Sorry," Moss offered.

At the same time, Judy said, "Oh, a little language never hurt anyone." Moss looked at them disapprovingly and they scoffed. "Sorry, Dad, but that guy just really got under my skin."

"Pretty sure that's his whole shtick," Moss offered. "You are just giving in to what he wants."

They took one more step forward in the line. They seemed to hardly be moving at all and the line stretched on further than Moss could see. "How long do we have to wait?"

"As long as it takes," Judy said, still fuming. "He said he'll get us a meeting?"

"Yeah," Moss nodded. "He will set it all up. Got into some of the shit the company pulls, pretty dark stuff."

"No shock there."

"And yet, here we are," Moss said, gesturing around the tunnel in which they waited.

"Look," Judy said, sounding genuinely annoyed that he kept bringing it up. "Is this place owned by an evil megacorporation? Sure. Does it also bring me joy? Yes.

"We are doing everything in our power to take these fuckers down, so let's at least take advantage of this while we can, okay?"

Moss shrugged and though he was busting their chops, he actually loved to see Judy so excited about something. They always seemed fine when they were working in their shop but here they seemed genuinely happy. And it was an odd lull time anyway. They had no leads to act on, Issy was still hospitalized and their meeting wouldn't be until later in the week.

While a whole bunch of things were looming, there was nothing pressing and Moss was happy to think that he could make one of his friends happy for a moment.

Smiling, and trying to take a different attitude, he asked, "So, what's the deal with this ride?"

Judy beamed, slapping him lightly on the chest with excitement.

"Can't this thing go any faster?" Moss whined as the cab flew them toward the clinic. They had spent most of the day at the amusement park, drinking, eating and going on rides. Moss pulled the gopher ears from his head and threw them to the floor of the cab.

"It's going as fast as its allowed to," Judy said, picking up the ears and dusting them off. They paused and cracked the slightest of smiles. "You used to be more fun."

"You used to be less," Moss shot back without even having to think, but he smiled. "To think that the least welcoming person is now one of my closest friends ..."

Judy let out a sardonic laugh. "To be fair, it's probably because I am really one of the few people left alive from back then."

"Now, ain't that a fucked-up truth," Moss said.

The cab banked and began to lower. As it did, the clinic came into view. It looked different; the windows were barred and a group of people with hoods pulled over their heads and masks covering their faces stood in front.

"The fuck is this?" Moss asked and Judy sighed.

"Assholes stealing drugs," they said. "With Carcer gone, the companies don't have its protection any longer. The mayor's new police force is trying to keep up but there is simply so much crime. These folks know that they have ample time to get in, steal the drugs and supplies and get out."

"Doesn't the building have security?" Moss asked in shock, terrified for Issy.

Judy shrugged as the cab dropped. "Sure, but not enough."

Moss gritted his teeth. "Solve one problem and create two more."

"Welcome to changing the world," they said, patting him on the back. "Just wait until we take down the entire AIC."

The idea sent Moss reeling but he shook his head to clear the thought and looked at the people as they set up tools to pull the bars from the window. Another knelt by the door, clearly trying to hack it before their friends had to cause a stir. There were six of them and Moss knew better than to simply start a firefight.

"We should wait," Judy cautioned.

"Right," Moss nodded, but the moment the cab touched down, he was out the door and moving toward the thieves.

"Moss," Judy stage-whispered after him but it was too late. His mind was made up.

The instincts that had carried him through so much flared and he walked right up to the thief closest to the quiet street. There was very little activity at this hour. A few people were gawking from apartment windows, but for the most part it was just Moss and the burglars. He walked right up and coldcocked the first one with the butt of his Kingfisher, sending him crashing to the ground.

The sound caused the others to turn and Moss immediately understood just how outnumbered he was. Crowbars, knives and brass knuckles appeared in a flash and they all seemed keen to start a fight. They were all dressed in a clichéd style that indicated they wanted to be perceived as tough — vests with spikes, fingerless leather gloves and heavy boots. Teeth and eyes exposed through holes in the masks shimmered in the neon lights of the shops.

"You picked the wrong people to mess with," said one, who Moss presumed was their leader.

Moss simply smiled and pointed his weapon, blasting the one who spoke with a blue beam that sent him to the ground in a vibrating pile. A large woman moved in, brandishing a lead pipe with curved elbow screwed to the end. She swung and Moss ducked quickly, sending the barrel of his beam pistol up into the woman's chin. She reeled back, staggered by the hit. This crew were clearly better at seeming than being tough.

All the rest of them stared in shock for a moment and then seemed to realize they should all attack at once. Moss's heart raced and he braced for the fight, happy that Stan had taken so much time in those early days to teach him how to fight.

As the three closed in on Moss, a fist met the side of one of their faces as Judy simply walked over and clocked him in the jaw. The thug turned and Judy landed two quick punches before swinging a leg and kicking him in the face. As the other two saw with shock what was happening, Moss shook his head and shot them both, the blue bolts flashing through and dropping them.

The last one looked up from the door in terror. "I'm — I'm sorry, guys," he muttered, holding his hands up. Moss was about to tell him to get out of there but Judy spoke first.

"You're good, finish what you are doing," they said. The kid and Moss both looked at them in confusion. Judy turned to Moss. "Building is on lockdown and the company won't unlock it until police arrive to secure the scene."

"Oh," Moss said, shaking his head and pointing his gun at the breaker. "Keep going."

"Sure, sure," he stammered. He was thin, terrified and had the wild eyes of a junkie. "Whatever you say." After a moment, the breaker turned back from his work and asked, "You guys think, once we in, I could …?"

"No!" Moss and Judy said in unison. It wasn't that they cared about protecting the interests of Crassun Emergency Services, but they didn't want to encourage this behavior.

Or so Moss told himself. It was hard for him to wrap his head around some of his own philosophies at this point. So many lines had become blurred. Dressed as he was in Robin Hood themed attire, he didn't know if the young people he had just knocked out were villains or heroes or something in between. They were acting out of selfishness, but it was based in a corrupt system designed to keep them oppressed. They were breaking into a business to steal, but it was from a subsidiary of a megacorporation which was part of the system that made it impossible for these people to better themselves.

"Or do," Moss amended and now the two looked at *him* in surprise. He turned to Judy, "He's stealing from a mega. What do we give a fuck for?"

"That outfit rubbing off on you?" Judy asked sarcastically as the breaker went back to his business, the corner of his mouth turned up in a smile.

Moss shrugged. "Maybe. Or maybe it's time I start really thinking about the world we are trying to make and the people we are trying to help."

"Should we not have beat the shit out of all of them?" Judy asked, gesturing to the people littering the sidewalk.

"I don't know. Maybe?"

"They might have hurt Issy."

"We wouldn't have," the kid said quietly.

"Shut the fuck up, no one asked you!" Judy snapped.

"Just saying," he muttered, getting back to work.

"You're going to be saying 'hi' to my fucking boot in a second," Judy said. "Get back to work. What's taking so long anyway?"

"I'm nervous," he told them, showing a shaking hand.

"You're nervous because I'm rushing you but stopping your work to make the point?" Judy said, their tone clear.

After another minute, the shutter over the door cranked open. The girl behind the counter stared at them in shock and terror.

"Oh, right," Moss said, seeing her. Looking at the kid, he said, "No stealing shit today. There is a person in here who will be blamed and probably lose her job."

"Huh?" the breaker said, standing. His hands were still shaking and sweat was beading on his forehead. His eyes had become redder and whatever drugs he had taken to work himself up to doing the robbery were now wearing off. His eye began to dart between Moss and the vending machine of drugs.

"No, man, don't," Moss said, seeing his mind.

"Fuck her!" the breaker said and rushed the door but before Moss could even point the Kingfisher, Judy had clotheslined the kid. As he rolled to get up, Moss shot him.

"I'm telling you," Judy said as they went to push the door open, "this change is going be really complicated. People trained by a brutal existence for generations are not just going to turn happily to altruism and a sense of society."

Watching the kid writhe on the ground, Moss said, "I have to believe we can change. We can all change for the better. For the betterment of ourselves and the world."

"The world?" Judy said. "This about animals again?"

Moss smiled. "In part," he said as they pushed the door open.

"Thanks," the girl behind the counter said. It came across as more of a question than a comment.

"You're welcome?" Judy said in what Moss thought was an unnecessarily mocking tone.

"Your friend will be out," the girl began, but the door hissed open and Moss saw Issy being pushed out from the back in a wheelchair, a medical drudge behind her. Moss ran over and wrapped his arms around Issy. She did not wince. She was feeling no pain. She kissed Moss on the neck.

"Oh, hi, Judy," she said with a childish grin.

"Hey, Is, how you holding up?"

"I'm so good, like, really so good," she said. "My mouth is dry though."

The drudge turned its metal faceplate to Moss. "I discharge her to you?"

"Yes," Moss said as the faceplate opened to reveal a screen and a spot for Moss to put the signature of whoever Patch had hacked in to pay for this. Pressing a finger to the screen, he signed for the service.

"I guess you own me now," Issy joked, giving Moss an exaggerated wink. "What are you going to do with me?" She tried to bat her eyelashes but couldn't pull it off, simply slow-blinking at Moss. He smiled.

"Put you to bed," he said.

"Oooooh, yes!" she grinned.

"We should be filming this for later," Judy mocked as Moss went around and took control of the wheelchair.

Issy swatted at Judy. "You dirty dog. Wanna watch the tape?"

"You are just a one-track mind right now," Moss said, unable to help himself from laughing. He had only seen her like this once before and it had amused him as much then as it did now. He also loved how mortified she would be later.

"Yes!" she exclaimed. "You can lay some track."

"That's not the expression." Moss laughed as he pushed her toward the door. As it opened and they pushed her toward the waiting cab up the street, Issy guffawed.

"Can you guys go anywhere without a trail of bodies?" She clapped her hands and kept laughing. "Can you imagine a real trail made out of bodies?" she asked, gazing up at Moss, who just grinned down at her. Judy had a small pocket drone filming Issy.

One of the thieves rolled over, grabbing his knife off the street. Moss had his Kingfisher out in a flash and shot him again. His body slumped to the sidewalk.

"Again! Again! Again!" Issy squealed in delight.

Judy laughed. "No wonder you were a company cop."

"Let's get you home," Moss said.

CHAPTER 10

"Is this a new friend?" Stu asked as it rolled into the room.

"Yes," Moss whispered. Issy was still technically awake, but it would have been hard to describe her as conscious. Her eyes rolled to the bot.

"Cute," she murmured.

"Got something," Patchwork said as he shadowed the door. "You and I need to talk."

Moss nodded.

"Good to see you back, Issy," Patch said with a smile.

"Hey, Willis," she said, glassy eyes opening just a moment. "Can I call you Willy?"

"No," Patchwork said, shaking his head and stepping from the room with Stu following.

Issy rolled to face away from Moss, pulling the blankets up to her neck and groaning.

Moss laid a hand on her back. "I love you," he told her softly. "And I'm sorry."

She shifted. "You always are," she said, and Moss stepped back. Though she was hardly there, the comment cut. He felt he was always apologizing to her. She had picked this life, too, had chosen to come with them; but he still felt responsibility for her.

Grunting, he stood and turned, closing the door softly and walking down the hallway to Patchwork's room. He had added more screens and computers. There was a small bed in one corner, but the space looked much more like a hacker's workshop than a personal space. Patch stamped out a cigarette, lit another one and looked up from his cartoon with a disapproving look.

"You know we need to talk, man," he scolded.

Moss hung his head. It was true. This program was getting dangerous, and although he didn't want to admit it, he knew he had to deal with it.

"I know."

"Like, it's one thing that you didn't bring Is, since she was, like, hospitalized but man, not bringing me, that's some cold action," Patchwork said, sounding sincerely hurt.

"Wait, what?" Moss asked.

"You went to D2Eland without me," he clarified, head hung hangdog.

Moss rolled his eyes. "You too with this shit?"

"It's just like, if you have a team outing, I would like to be invited," he said quietly.

"Me too!" Stu announced from the floor. "I would also like to be part of a a group of players forming one side in a competitive game or sport."

"Pretty sure it's no droids allowed," Moss said.

"I see what you did there," Patch said.

Moss stepped forward and put a hand on Patchwork's shoulder. "I am sorry. For one thing, you were busy; and secondly, I had no clue this was such a big deal for everyone."

"Really?"

"Yeah," Moss said. "ThutoCo had in-house programming to keep us insulated. I've only seen a few of the animated movies you guys are on about as part of the film education Gibbs prescribed for me."

"Oh," Patch said.

"I *am* sorry I didn't invite you," Moss said.

"Thanks."

"But I'll admit to being a bit surprised. I mean, the megas sent your mom to war for no good reason, and now you want to give them an absurd amount of money for some old ride that gives you a crick in your neck?"

"Oh, no, man," Patch laughed. "You are looking at it all wrong. D2E owns all the best properties. My favorite superheroes and scifi movies."

"But didn't they corrupt those things you love?" Moss asked, actually interested.

Patchwork shrugged. "Yes and no. Sure, they made some of it more family friendly, but they also just made more of it and took risks to keep and get new fans. It's a mixed bag."

"Well, they are evil too," Moss told him flatly. "I met with Rude Von 'Tude and he filled me in a bit."

"Oh, man, that dude's hilarious," Patch said. "Fucked up but funny as shit."

"Judy had a different take."

"Oh, for sure. He's a terrible human being. But still…"

"Funny as shit?"

"That's the one," Patch smirked. After a pause, he smiled with realization. "Kinda a metaphor. He is like D2E itself. Like, he is a bad person who does bad shit, but I still like him for the entertainment he provides me."

"Gray area's getting ubiquitous."

"The fuck else is new?"

Moss chuckled.

"Now," Patch said, and his face grew dark. "What the actual fuck, man?"

He shook his head. Moss could see it wasn't anger but pure disappointment.

"One thing if you were avoiding it but straight up lying, that's fucked."

"I know," Moss said. "I think I kept hoping if I left it alone long enough it would go away."

"For a smart guy, that's pretty dumb," Patch observed.

"I'll cop to that."

Patch gestured for Moss to take a seat in the chair to his left, surrounded by dangling cords and cables. They had been at this one safe house long enough that they had all really settled in and made the place their own. They had started to know the neighborhood and even furnish the place a bit. Patch had this whole rig that could be used for VR gaming or to look into Moss's head.

Moss sat down and took a deep breath.

"We can up the dose of the dampeners too," Patch offered.

"More drugs," Moss said in disappointment.

"Or you could come off them and see how long it takes for ThutoCo to hack your brain again," Patchwork snapped. "Or," he said as Moss leaned back in the chair, "you could uninstall it."

Moss shook his head. Patchwork only mentioned this once in a very great while, but it pissed Moss off every time. "We need it. I can do things with that program that even you can't do with your entire rig. We need to keep it at our disposal."

"You are like a guy sitting on a pile of uranium, saying that we could use it as a nuke while his skin melts," Patch said, shaking his head.

"Also," Moss said quietly.

Patchwork nodded. "You dad is in there."

"Yeah," Moss said. He couldn't stand the idea that he could lose the AI construct of his father that his parents had created and hidden from the world. "I know it's stupid but it's important. The combination of the potential power and the sentimental importance . . . I just can't delete it. Not until after we take down ThutoCo."

"I get it. I mean, you are talking to the world's biggest momma's boy."

He smiled and Moss laughed. "Guess that's true."

"Okay, gonna run some analytics on the hardware and soft," he said. "The neural mesh system could be degrading. They use the off-world materials, but I know that sometimes it can be an actual problem with the chip and neural lace. If not, then it's just the same old problem we have been having..." he paused a moment as he stared at imaging.

"So, you and Tak ..." Moss said.

"You really want to get into who I'm fucking right now?" Patch didn't look at Moss, he just looked at the display as a doctor would.

Moss shrugged. "It's better than thinking about the option of having either a malfunctioning program in my mind or melting alien metals in my brain."

"It technically isn't metal in the traditional sense," Patch said. "And me and Tak are just having fun. But it's been a minute, so that's cool."

"Good," Moss said. "I'm happy for you. We should all take time to enjoy life from time to time or we will all end up like..." but he let the words fall.

"Oh, shit," Patch said.

"What?" Moss asked in alarm.

"Just got a crazy flare up," he said. "I don't know how to describe it in dumbass terms but it was like a programming explosion."

"Guess that means it's not the hardware," Moss suggested hopefully.

"For sure," Patch agreed. "So it's the same old shit with the program. Sorry, man."

Moss sighed. He felt like he sighed a lot these days. "I think the other option seems to be worse, so I'll take the devil I know."

"Sure," Patchwork said and stepped around in front of Moss, their eyes connecting. "But listen to me. I tell you this now. Getting knocked out of your chair by a program in your brain is crazy shit. You lose consciousness even once because of this, I'm gonna pull the plug. I'm gonna uninstall the whole thing."

"But . . ." Moss began to protest and Patch took another drag.

Holding up a hand, curling wisps dancing off the cigarette, Patchwork said, "No, this is not optional. It knocks you out, it's coming out. Not worth it anymore."

Moss nodded. He knew he could fight, make the point that it was his mind and his choice to bear the risk, but he didn't want to. He also didn't want to let this thing kill him for a weapon he might never use and a program with a digital dad he no longer accessed.

Judy popped their head in. "You expecting a call?"

Moss shook his head.

"Gil is on for you, put it up in the," they waved a hand, "you know, meeting room place."

"Get some rest," Moss said.

Judy cracked a smirk. "I will when you do."

"I will after the call," Moss said and turned to Patchwork. "Unless?"

"Not time sensitive," he told them. "I mean, except in the way all of the information is at the moment."

"Got it," Moss said. "I'll take this call and check back."

"And rest," Patch and Judy said simultaneously before looking at one another and smiling.

A holoprojection of Gil from The Conservation was in the middle of the room, the hologram a translucent recreation of the man in his uniform. He looked older than he was in Moss's memory, but Moss realized that they all probably looked a lot older after the past few years.

"Hey, Gil!" Moss said.

"Hello there, Moss," the man greeted him with a small smile. "Sorry it has taken so long to get back to you. I know you have wanted to chat."

"I have," Moss said, feeling like he had so many questions for Gil. "But first, how's Amy?"

Gil smiled. "She's great," he said. "She joined the team on an expedition recently and is starting to get involved with some proper animal care."

"What's that, like picking up shit?" Moss asked half-jokingly.

"Pretty much, actually," he said, chuckling, and then asked hopefully, "Is Anders with you? She wanted me to make sure I said hi for her and tell him to stop by soon."

Moss felt like he wanted to vomit. The death of his grandmother had absorbed his thoughts so profoundly that it was hard to remember Anders had been killed too. It had been so close and so violent that Moss tried with all his might to keep it from the forefront of his mind.

"Oh," Moss said, nearly choking on the word. "He, um, well, it's like, he . . . " Moss tried to force the words.

"I see," Gil said softly. "I'm sorry for your loss."

"Me too for you," Moss offered. "He was a good man."

"Truly," Gil agreed, and Moss could hear the heartbreak in the man's voice. "All the good ones die."

Moss nodded. "And yet, here we are."

"Here we are." The two men were silent for a long moment, contemplating the way of the world.

"She'll be okay when you tell her?" Moss asked, thinking about the sweet little girl he had met.

Gil's face grew dark. "She'll be fine. Honestly, she will," he told Moss sincerely. "Thing is, she sees death all the time. The animals, the people we send out . . . death is a part of her life in a way no father wishes for his child."

Moss nodded and Gil continued. "On one hand, it's important for her to grow accustomed to it, desensitized to it, but on the other, I hate it. All the work we do is for the love of life, all life, and if the next generation grows up without that love or with a callus over its collective heart, we are doomed."

"It's a delicate balance."

"Precisely. But I will send her your best."

"Please," Moss said and decided to change the subject. His exhaustion was now catching up with him. It was easy to keep up his energy when things needed to happen, but now, discussing hard topics, he just wanted some rest. "And I assume you heard the news from the Scubas?"

Gil nodded slowly. "No surprise there."

"Yeah?" Moss asked.

"We have done extensive particulate studies and all but proved it wasn't toxic on the surface," Gil said. "But when it came time to test the hypothesis, I never approved it. I was not willing to risk the lives of one of my people to prove it because, if we were wrong, if there was some agent we hadn't detected, one of my people would die a horrible, brutal death."

"Could have told us," Moss said. "We have no shortage of people we would have been happy to test a potentially brutal death on."

Gil shook his head and did not seem to find the implication amusing in the least. "You and I are in different businesses."

"Apologies," Moss amended quickly. "But I do want to talk to you a bit about the future of our planet."

"You believe you are that close?" Gil asked, looking surprised.

Moss laughed. "Oh, no, but we are moving in that direction and I would like to have as many things in place as possible. If we are able to rid the planet of the megas and try to return to some semblance of a harmonious existence with the wild, what does that look like?"

Gil sat back wherever he was, the receiver losing him a moment before correctly projecting him into the room.

"This is a loaded question, Moss. You must understand, it is not as simple as one might think. There are so many factors, and I will try to help you to understand, but it is not going to be possible in one conversation. I will have one of my people send you a folio with a much deeper plan."

"Thank you," Moss said, but he was already worried that the next part of the plan would really be the hardest part. If they somehow destroyed the AIC and rid the planet, or even just this part of the planet, of the companies, there would still be so much to do.

"What you need to understand first is that there are a lot of people on this planet," Gil said. "Not just that they all produce waste and require electricity and water which can be sustainably achieved with some difficulty, but they also need to eat. We reached a critical mass and without the advent of prophet root, starvation would have driven us into extinction if climate change had not.

"ThutoCo did solve *that* problem, but, of course they solved it in ways which hurt a lot of people. The Great Pandemic killed off huge swaths of earth's population. As you would expect, poor countries got hit much harder than richer.

"This helped with one part of the problem as there were fewer mouths to feed. The root itself also helped heal the planet and with feeding the remaining people. In fairness to Wesley Grayson, it was a remarkable thing … if it hadn't also come at such high cost."

"Some death is the price of all life." Moss said the old ThutoCo company line for the first time in a long time.

"Certainly true, in its own way," Gil said. "But the cost was greater than just that of human life. Once the humans were forced into the cities, the company took over most of the space in between. It wasn't just that they clear cut so much of the continent, but that they also demolished tens of thousands of towns. This immense, dangerous waste has been piled on top of the remains of the cities that fell.

"There are the endless fields of crops, active cities belching toxicity and decimated ones. Simply destroying megacorp control doesn't inherently solve anything. There are still many issues."

"Can't we just pull the roots and return the space to the animals?" Moss asked, he would later think quite naively.

Gil shook his head. "There are several things to consider. First, the people on the planet will still need to eat and most of the foodstuffs on earth are based on P-root. Second, most industries are based on materials provided by the off-world colonies and those supplies are traded for with the root since so few planets can sustain fields like earth does.

"The last and perhaps most important part is that once you tell the world that The Betweens are not toxic, they may not want to stay in the cities. They could, and likely will, decide that it is better outside. Once they do, we may be faced with the same problem we had before The Great Pandemic —that human spread is more devastating to the natural world than the root."

"Right," Moss said. "If we can keep the people out, or in, as it were, you have the samples and seeds to return parts of the world to its natural state?"

Gil chuckled and Moss felt like a total idiot, overwhelmed by the reality of what was next to come. They had been so focused for so long on victory that they had not spent enough time considering what they would do if they actually won.

"This is where there is some good news and some bad," he told Moss. "There is actually much more natural world left than you might think, and while it seems like the fields stretch on forever, nature has reclaimed quite a bit since people were forced within the walls. If you simply tear up all the fields, replant and allow growth, the planet will return to nature. But it will not ever be as it was. Different seeds will spread and different wildlife will disseminate.

"Will it be better? Sure. Will Mother Nature be able to breathe once more? Yes. Will it be the earth that was? No."

Moss thought about what Gil had said. There were so many factors Moss had not yet taken into account; and by his own admission, this was only a watered-down version of the problems they would face.

"Don't spin, though," Gil said with a smile. "If you can tear down the megacorps, we can do *a lot* of good for the planet.

We can help a lot of wildlife and find a way to sustain human life. Of course . . ." he trailed off.

"What?"

"We will need help."

"Money?"

Gil shrugged. "If that is what you plan to use in the next iteration, yes."

"You will have everything you need."

Then Moss tilted his head, thinking about The Conservation, the vast building with staff and what had appeared to be state-of-the-art facilities. "Where do you get your funding now?"

For the briefest of moments, Moss saw a look of concern flash across Gil's face before he regained himself and said, "Our underground operation has many underground benefactors." He gave a little wink.

"Ours too. But ours are being killed."

Gil grimaced. "You should probably sort that out."

"I'm trying," he said. "But first I need to get some rest."

"Right," Gil said. "Brain functionality is directly related to sleep patterns."

"I know, I know."

"Anyway, it was nice chatting with you and let's talk more soon," Gil said.

"Yes. I am sure I will have a million more questions."

Gil smiled. "And I'm sure I will have a million answers for each one."

"Send Amy my best, will you?" Moss added, circling back to the beginning of the call.

"Will do. And keep up the good work. I know Anders was proud to be a part of what you were doing."

Moss swallowed his emotions as the projection faded. He needed sleep. Then he needed to find out who was killing the people who were helping him..

CHAPTER 11

Moss sipped his coffee, feeling like his brain had returned a bit after sleeping. It had not been restful at first. Issy had snored like a chainsaw and his mind had raced thinking of everything that had happened; but once he had fallen asleep, it had been a sleep like death. The sun was already threatening to set by the time he awakened, and even Issy was out of bed.

Patchwork stepped into the room with Stu hot on his heels.

"Joined the land of the living, I see."

Moss nodded and rubbed his face. Patch turned his attention to Issy. "Nice to see you out of bed too."

Issy smiled and stretched, arching her back and groaning. She looked like a cat getting up from a sunny spot on the floor.

"It's nice to be back," she said with a smile.

Moss was pleased that she already seemed to be her old self. She would always have her scars, but the road to recovery was short.

"And now I'm ready for action," she added.

Moss and Patchwork both stared at her in surprise.

"What?" she asked in annoyance, as though she didn't know what their objections were.

Judy chuckled as they stepped into the room. "If she says she's ready to go, she's ready to go."

"Thank you, Judy," Issy said gratefully.

"Oh," Judy amended. "Don't take what I say as an endorsement of what you are doing. Just know you have my emotional support."

Issy rolled her eyes theatrically. "Well, I guess that'll have to do."

"If everybody's ready . . ." Patch said.

They all followed him into the next room and sat on the couches. Patchwork turned off the lights and brought up a 3-D display of a room. He turned to Stu. "I think it's better if you don't see this."

"I don't *see*," Stu said to Patchwork. "I have cameras that collect data which my processors analyze." Then, after a pause, it added, "though I suppose when you think about it, that is pretty similar to what human eyesight is."

"Either way, it's probably best if you go somewhere else for this," Patchwork said in such a sweet tone that it really sounded like he was talking to a living thing.

"Why don't you go look for Perro and see what she's up to?" Moss suggested.

"Perro translates to dog," Stu said. Then, when nobody answered it, the bot rolled from the room. Patchwork quickly closed the door behind it.

"I was able to pull the footage from Stu's memory," Patchwork said grimly.

A holoprojected AR overlay enveloped the room and at once the space was Rigg's apartment. A playback began and they all watched as Rigg stepped through the frame and began walking to his workstation with a bowl in his hand. A loud knock caused them all to startle.

"Oh," Patchwork said, "I should actually mute this. What's fucked is that Stu's digital screams are more traumatizing than those of the man about to be killed. Also, you guys don't need to watch all of this. It's pretty ugly."

Patchwork used his neural link to fast-forward the footage until the door was eventually kicked in by armored agents that looked the same as the ones that had shot Issy. Moss felt his heart rate increase just seeing them and he laced his fingers through Issy's. But when he looked at her, he didn't see fear but anger and determination.

As the agents moved towards Rigg, Patchwork paused the footage, tilting and zooming in on a barcode and serial number that had been scratched out.

"As you can see," Patchwork said with a grin of pride, "the makers of this armor have been removed. But if you look closely, you'll see that the person who customized this armor left a small attribution mark next to the old barcode."

"Why would they do that?" Issy asked.

"I asked myself the same thing, but then I decided to ask some friends." He seemed to pause for theatrical effect. "Long story short, artists who take pride in their work sign it."

"How do we find this artist?" Moss asked.

Once again, Patchwork beamed with pride. "Way ahead of you," he said, and the display turned from the interior of Rigg's apartment to a city street. Shops lined both sides, the usual open stalls hawking merch to passing locals.

"It's a good news, bad news situation," Patchwork explained.

He stepped into the middle of the display and pointed to a store selling holiday goods all year round. Toy trains circled presents under the tree in the window and life-sized Nutcracker statues stood beside the door. A machine sprayed soap bubbles out the shop door in an imitation of snow, and an old man roasted chestnuts on a flat, heated disk.

"The armorer's office is behind this shop front," Patchwork informed them finally.

Judy stood up, looked around the room, and said, "I have to take a shit." They stomped from the room and Moss furrowed his brows, knowing that it was just a cover.

"You can keep going," Moss told him, and Patchwork obliged.

" I told you that was the good news or maybe I didn't. But that was the good news, that I had the address." He paused a moment. "The street is under the protection of The Legion."

Moss let out a loud and annoyed grunt. "Didn't we kill all those guys?"

Patchwork laughed. "It's cute that you think taking down one chapter would destroy the entire gang."

Issy patted Moss on the head like a dog. "It really *is* cute," Issy said, but she couldn't cover her condescension.

"Fine. Whatever. I'm just really fucking sick of these guys," Moss said. "They have been a constant thorn in my side since literally the moment I got to B.A. City."

"Well, what do you expect in a city half-run by gangs?" Patchwork said with a laugh.

Issy stood and put her hands on her hips. "Well, no time like the present."

Moss opened his mouth but paused. He wanted to tell her that there was no way she was going into another firefight, but he knew the decision wasn't his to make and that even by suggesting it she was more likely to come. All he wanted was to keep her safe, but this was the life she had chosen and that he had encouraged her to choose.

Issy seemed to read his mind and gave him a disparaging look. "I'm a big girl," she said.

"It's not that," Moss answered, letting his head drop. "It's that you were *just* shot. I had to watch you be wheeled into a hospital room, and I just don't want to have to see it again."

"Well, that's sounds like a personal problem," Issy said and laughed as she patted him on the cheek. She turned to look at Patchwork. "You coming?"

He looked at her in surprise. "I'm not usually asked to come along."

"Yeah, well, it was Sandra who always wanted to keep you safe for your mommy, but if I can get shot and go back to work the next day, I think you can face down a couple of hopped-up bikers with us."

"Sounds good," Patchwork said. But his voice quavered with either nerves or excitement. Moss wished Gibbs and Ynna were here to help. Issy was great in a fight but had just been hurt, and Patchwork had a great many skills but was still not very experienced in combat.

As Patchwork left the room to get geared up, Issy turned to look at Moss. "I really do appreciate your looking out for me," she said and gave him that smile that always melted his heart. "But you need me now."

"I know," Moss admitted. And it really was true. "There are just times when…"

The silence hung for just a moment before Issy filled in, "When we really need Sandra."

"Yes," Moss said. It came out so quietly that it was almost just a breath.

She looked at him, trying to cover the concern written all over her face. "I know we've talked a little bit about it, but you know I'm always here if you need me."

"Thanks," he said and then laughed, deciding to change the subject. "Did Judy show you the videos from last night?"

Issy scrunched her face. "There are videos?"

Moss laughed. "Oh, there are videos."

Moss, Issy and Patchwork walked slowly down the street. By the time they were ready, the sun was beginning to set, making Moss feel he had slept the entire day away.

Stu had told them that Judy had grabbed a coat and left the safe house and when Moss tried to communicate, they did not answer. He knew there was more there, but it would have to wait.

Like most market streets in the city, this one was abuzz with activity. People pushed past each other to get from one stall to another, to grab something on their way to or from work or to meet a friend. There seemed to be a deal going down in every nook and cranny, and Moss even saw a person sending out delivery drones from their second-story apartment. As usual, ads blared everywhere — jingles here, sales pitches there and holograms hocking wares.

"Bet you're pretty happy that I blocked those HackAds, eh?" Patchwork said with a laugh. "You would have so many strip club ads popping up in your brain that you wouldn't be able to see straight."

"What was that?" Issy asked, sounding more amused than angry.

"Nothing," Moss hissed. "Let's stay focused."

"Oh, *now* you want to stay focused," Patchwork mocked, "but we had all the time in the world when we passed that pet shop and you wanted to play with the kittens."

"Hey, after talking to Gil today, I thought it was important that I reconnect with animals," Moss justified halfheartedly.

"Oh, sure, you keep telling yourself that," Issy said, and she and Patchwork shared a look and then a laugh.

In a strange way, to Moss it felt similar to when he was hanging out with Ynna and Gibbs and he was happy for the camaraderie. Things had been so tough, so exhausting after everything had gone down on election night, that it was nice that things were starting to return to some semblance of normal.

"Now is probably as good a time as any," Issy said, nodding in the direction of a staircase. It led down to the basement door, walled off on either side by low bricks and bags of garbage. Moss ducked into the alley and padded down the stairs, but stopped before the landing. It was covered in a few centimeters of liquid, the smell of which instantly told him it was human piss.

Stripping off the clothes he had on, he rolled them up and popped them in a bag, setting it in the least urine-covered part of the staircase. He pulled a mask over his face and felt the Dermidos shimmer to life. Looking down, his hand all but disappeared except when he made quick movements. His Kingfisher was jammed under the suit, and though it bulged and pressed painfully into his back, it was hidden.

He walked back up the stairs and tapped Issy on her ugly-sweater clad shoulder. It was bright red with LED lights flashing from green lettering reading "Holiday Cheer Officer." Moss had not been able to stop laughing when she had put it on. He had begun to cry from laughter as Patchwork emerged from his room wearing a fuzzy blue sweater with bright yellow puffballs and an image of Stan the Gopher in a holiday hat bearing the words "Double Your Cheer With Holiday Magic" in a swirly font.

"I'll be right behind you," Moss whispered and the two nodded, heading toward the store. Moss had only known The Holiday from celebrations at ThutoCo, but Sandra had taught him that it was one of the last vestiges of a pre-pandemic monotheistic religious holiday which itself was a remnant of some ancient polytheistic religious holiday. Over time, the megas had stripped away the spiritual aspects and replaced them entirely with consumer faith until it was little more than a day off work to exchange goods.

As he stepped onto the sidewalk, following Issy and Patchwork, he felt a bit ridiculous. Though he knew he was invisible to the naked eye, walking around on the street in a skintight Dermidos and nothing else was odd.

The door to the store was like a gateway into another world. Toys chirped, clashed, danced, and sang as machines blew bubbles into the air, lights twinkled, and chamber music played at an oppressive volume. The man behind the counter was old and fat and sported a white beard. He wore red and white hat that tapered to the end with a pom-pom. Clearly, he was trying to resemble the man depicted on half of the items.

"Ho – Ho – hello," the man bellowed gleefully as they walked in.

Playing the part, Issy greeted, "Hello! Happy Holiday!"

"And don't we just wish it was The Holiday all year round?" the man asked. He plucked a plate of cookies off the counter and thrust them forward from across the store. Issy and Patch didn't need to be asked twice and bounded past the toys and trinkets straight for the cookies. They both took bites and made happy, contented eating sounds as Moss slinked through the space.

Being invisible didn't mean he would be reckless. He made his way slowly through the racks, careful not to touch anything or jangle any toys. If there was a freelance armorer behind the store, there was sure to be more than toy soldiers guarding the place. However, there were a lot of toy soldiers lining the walls.

"I do wish it was The Holiday season all year round," Issy enthused. "It really is the one time of year when everybody is kind to one another."

That made the fat man really happy, and he beamed at them. "Is there something in particular you're looking for, or just browsing?"

As Issy answered, Moss crept toward the counter. It was partitioned by little more than a piece of wood that could be flipped up and Moss crouched slowly, careful that his knees didn't crack as he did so. Sliding under the counter, his heart began to race. As a song blasted about how it was the most wonderful time of the year, Moss skulked towards the door labeled "Employees Only."

Now, he told Issy neurally.

Nothing happened.

He tried again.

But Issy just kept talking to the man behind the counter, distracting him. Neural communication was down. That only reinforced the idea that there was more to the shop than met the eye, and there was a lot that met the eye.

He would have to do it himself and just hope that the man didn't notice. Reaching up, he put a hand on the doorknob, and slowly opened the door. He didn't take his eyes off the jolly man, who neither turned nor took any notice of Moss as he sneaked into the back.

Sighing, he turned towards the employee's space and was greeted with the muzzle of a gun. A woman dressed as a Holiday elf with one black cybernetic eye stared at him and said, "Santa, someone's trying to sneak down your chimney."

CHAPTER 12

Moss didn't waste any time. He blasted his body forward, grabbing the gun as it discharged into the ceiling. As always seemed to happen with new technology, this next-generation Demidos was no longer state-of-the-art. Someone had cracked the code, and now it no longer provided the invisibility it once did. Of course, he had to find out this way.

The elf headbutted him and he turned to take it on the cheek. Santa had grabbed Patchwork by the throat, but he had misjudged the real threat and Issy had wheeled a roundhouse kick that had landed squarely on the side of his head.

Moss staggered back, still gripping the beam gun and pointed it away from his body. The elf fired again, the heat of the weapon burning his hands through his gloves before the bolt blasted a chunk out of the wall, spraying the two of them with dust and debris.

As Moss charged shoulder-first toward the elf, Issy popped over the counter, knocking Santa to the ground. He, too, pulled out a gun and wildly fired a burst, bullets spraying throughout the building. He wasn't seeing straight and missed; Issy dodged easily out of the way as Patchwork ducked. Patch's eye went black and the digital toys around the store began hopping off the shelves, making their way quickly toward Santa.

Issy leapt through the door, pulling the elf off Moss and throwing her against the wall. Santa began shooting at the toys as they moved around him. Fluff, stuffing, and electronics exploded all over the room, but there were too many of them. Large, small, loud and quiet, the toys jumped all over Santa, stabbing, poking and generally assaulting him. He screamed and thrashed as the toys began to destroy him.

The elf tried to kick Issy, but she blocked it with ease and landed a punch right on her nose. Moss pulled the Kingfisher from his Dermidos and blasted the elf. She slumped to the ground as Patchwork made his way back to them.

"One helluva Black Friday stampede there," he joked, hooking a thumb in the direction of the destroyed Santa.

Issy made a face. "Poor taste."

"Yeah," Patchwork admitted, "I think I've been listening to too much Rude Von 'Tude."

"Still hard to believe he's on our side," Issy observed.

"Being on the side of right and being a good person are not the same thing," Moss noted.

This had been a hard-learned lesson for him and this time, for some reason, he saw it coming. Closing his eyes, he braced for the mental impact. He felt the strike from inside his brain but didn't let it knock him down. He gritted his teeth, balled his fists and felt it, but didn't allow it to best him.

Exhaling slowly, he was happy he was wearing a mask so that neither of the other two could tell what just happened. But Issy was still looking at his dust-covered form with a look of concern. He knew he would hear about this later.

Pulling off the mask, he said, "Okay, we gotta keep moving. They must've called reinforcements and I doubt that our toy army can hold off a motorcycle gang for long."

"I don't know, man," Patch laughed. "An army of blood-covered toys might send me running for the hills."

They stepped through the narrow concrete hallway that opened into a square cement room with a plastic table and chairs set in the middle. A coffee pot burbled quietly on a countertop and a TV on mute flashed in the corner, but there was no sign of a secret hideout.

Moss turned to Patchwork, but the kid's eye was already black, clearly scanning the room for whatever hidden compartment lay within. He strode to the sink and flipped the tap to show that it didn't do anything. He opened the little cupboard under the sink and there it was: a big open space with a ladder leading downward.

Moss laughed and asked, "What percentage of buildings in this city have hidden spaces?"

"It really does feel like all of them," Patchwork agreed.

"Yeah, but that's only because we deal with the underside of society. We are not going into normal people's houses. We're dealing almost exclusively with people with something to hide. Ourselves included," Issy said with a hint of superiority.

Standing beside the opening, Patch gestured down the ladder. "Just because I found it doesn't mean I'm going down there first."

Moss nodded and stepped over. "Out of the frying pan…"

"Our life is nothing but frying pans," Issy said as Moss turned and began to climb down the ladder.

As he descended into the dark, he wondered what would be waiting for him at the bottom. It was possible that the workshop below had a video feed from the main store and the armorer would be waiting for him with a weapon primed. Or it could be booby-trapped. Or there could be a gang down there.

He craned his neck as the light from the bottom began to grow and stopped just before his feet crossed the threshold into the space below. Scrunching his body, he tried to tilt and look into the space, but there wasn't enough room and he ended up hitting his head on the cement. The hole didn't appear deep, so he turned and let go, dropping into the space with his weapon pointed out.

For once, he was pleasantly surprised.

The workshop was full of tools and supplies, pieces of armor and weapons, work benches and mechanized assistants. It was Judy's dream, and Moss was disappointed that they weren't here to enjoy it — or more likely steal from it.

The armorer himself was hunched over a piece of plate metal, working away with a natural left hand, a cybernetic right hand, and two long metal cybernetics protruding from a plate built into his back. He wore tiny old headphones, two soft pads connected by a strand of metal that went over his head and attached by a cord to some circular player.

As they could still hear the music from upstairs through all that distance, Moss understood why the man wanted to escape into his headphones. The three friends nodded at each another, and Moss and Issy pointed their weapons at the man as Patchwork's eye went black. All at once, the armorer's metal parts went limp and he jumped out of his seat, turning to face them as he flipped up his face covering. His coveralls bore the name Gav stitched into the front.

His eyes were wide with terror, but he tried to cover it up with a tough face. "What you want?"

"We're interested in some work that you did," Moss said. "All you need to do is tell us who paid you and we will be on our way."

The man shook his head and tried to puff himself up, but with his flaccid cybernetics, he just looked weak. "Telling you that would be my death sentence."

Issy took a step forward. "Not telling us will be your death sentence."

Again, he tried to look tough and again it failed. Scrawny and dirty, and in torn green coveralls, the man was anything but an imposing sight.

"I ain't telling you anything, and when The Legion gets here —"

But Moss didn't let him finish. He was sick of getting the runaround, sick of being stalled, sick of having to track down leads and not getting answers, sick of all of it. He stepped forward, grabbed the man's shirt collar, and jammed his Kingfisher in the man's face. He flipped the beam to lethal and said, "Tell us what we want to know or die."

"Oh, oh, okay," Gav said, raising his hand defensively. "What's the piece? I'll tell you! I'll tell you!"

Patchwork hacked one of the holoprojectors and instantly a depiction of the armored assassin that had killed Rigg appeared in the middle of the room.

"Oh, no, not that," Gav said in terror. "Please, don't make me tell you. They really will kill me."

With his free hand, Moss gripped one of the man's fingers and bent it upwards towards the wrist until it cracked. The man shrieked. It wasn't just the pain, but Moss was also affecting his livelihood, which waswhat he was going for.

"You didn't have to do that!" Gav shrieked. "It was D2E," he whimpered, tucking his hand between his legs, the

119

self-soothing action more difficult because of his cybernetics. "It was D2E," he repeated.

"See?" Moss said with a smile. "That wasn't so hard, now was it?"

"Ice cold," Patchwork observed, as Gav continued to back away, terror all over his face.

"Think we should let him live?" Issy asked. Moss knew it was just an intimidation tactic, but Patchwork looked appalled.

Ignoring the look, Moss answered, "Not if he forgets our faces."

Gav backed into one of his tables, knocking over whatever he had been working on. "I really don't know who you guys are, and I'll definitely forget your faces. Please, just let me live. I have a family."

"Everyone has a fucking family," Moss told the man harshly. "But we will take you at your word."

There was no reason to hurt this man any further. He had given them what they came for. Moss was a bit surprised that it was D2E, but he was starting to understand that this company was gunning for them too.

As they turned to leave, the ground above them began to shake. The Legion must have arrived.

Moss turned to Gav. "Where's the secret exit?"

"I – I – don't –"

Moss moved forward like a tiger ready to strike, staring at the remaining unbroken fingers. The armorer backed away and bumped into his table again.

"Okay, okay," and Gav gestured toward a patch of brickwork as he reached under one of the tables and pressed a button. The bricks rumbled and split, and the three of them made their way into the tunnel, lit with obviously pilfered

Holiday lights blinking red and green. They moved quickly as the door closed behind them.

They knew they didn't have much time. Regardless of what the man said, Moss knew he would sic The Legion on them the second their henchmen showed up at his workshop. They needed to get out of here quickly. The tunnel wound on and on, leading them toward some unknown destination. It wasn't long before they heard the door reopen and voices shouting behind them.

"Maybe we should have killed him," Issy joked.

The lights ended at a carved-out opening in the wall with some metal pressed against it

"Issy, cover us," Moss said, gesturing down the hallway where they had come from. He waved Patchwork over to help him push. They both put their shoulders into it and heaved, Moss's cybernetic legs activating and making short work of what turned out to be a dumpster. They pushed it aside and Moss sighed as he stepped around it.

"Surprise, motherfuckers," a leather-clad biker said.

There were several of them, their bikes parked behind with lights pointing at the dumpster, blinding Moss. He immediately regretted not turning his Dermidos back on. Through the glare, Moss could see the barrels of many weapons.

Behind him, he heard Issy's weapon discharge and people scream. In a moment, she emerged as well, stopped beside Patchwork, and said, "Oh, shit."

Moss was sad this would be his end but happy it would be quick. He had been in so many situations that would have killed him slowly but getting shot by a gang would mean he would die before he even realized it. That was something, anyway.

Then, the ganger who had spoken exploded, blood spraying everywhere before his body was propelled to the ground. Moss lifted his weapon and fired into the back of another as the gangers turned to face the oncoming threat. Another rifle cracked and another Legion member fell to the ground.

The next few moments were a blur. More backlit blood sprayed into the air. The rattle of machine gun fire rang out. Then Issy's weapon sang. One of the bikes revved and careened forward, smashing into one of the gangers. Another one screamed and Moss saw more blood spray as a figure stepped forward.

"You would think," a familiar voice said, "that these idiots would stop coming after us because we kill them. Every. Single. Time."

Ynna chuckled as she stepped forward and dramatically blew the smoke from the barrel of her SMG. "It is not like we just kill them, we decimate them every single time. I mean, kill them in droves, really. I just don't get it," she said and shrugged.

Moss and Issy ran forward and embraced Ynna as Patchwork stood still as a statue. "Welcome back. Thank you," the two said, but Ynna just smirked.

"Yeah, it's a good thing Seti was keeping such close tabs on you ding-dongs," Ynna mocked.

Gibbs made his way over from wherever he had been, his long rifle slung over his shoulder.

"Aaaaand we're back," he said in imitation of something, and Moss ran over to hug him, happier than he had ever been in his life to see someone.

"Welcome back," Moss said with a smile. "That was really good timing."

Ynna laughed. "Pretty sure that no matter when we came back," she said, "we would've found you guys in a firefight."

Moss and Issy nodded and Moss said, "You're right about that."

CHAPTER 13

Back at the safe house, Moss, Issy and Patch filled Gibbs and Ynna in on everything that had happened.

"Sounds like a whole bunch of nothing," Ynna joked.

"Yeah," Gibbs agreed. "Without us, the only thing these guys can do is get shot."

"Ooh, too soon, Gibby," Issy laughed, throwing a bottlecap at him.

They were sprawled on couches and on the floor or milling around. Finding out D2E was behind the attacks just meant it was more pressing to take the company down; but they didn't have much to go on. Once Moss had his meeting, they would know how D2E was tracking them and put a stop to it. But for the moment, it left them with nothing pressing to do. Plus, after several action filled days, they were all happy to relax and spend some time together.

"Where's Judy?" Ynna asked. "I assumed they were just in the room, but they're nowhere to be found."

"They made a quick escape after the last briefing," Moss explained. "Seemed like it was something to do with the Holiday."

"Ah," Ynna said, plopping down on the couch.

Moss looked at her expectantly. "Well, are you going to explain?"

"No," Ynna said and popped a beer with her cybernetic hand.

"I love how you didn't bring me one of those," Gibbs said as he shook his empty beer bottle at Ynna.

"Don't want you getting fat," Ynna said with a wink. "Go get it yourself."

"And, Moss, while you're up, grab me one, too" Issy said.

Moss looked at her in confusion. "I wasn't getting up," but when she gave him a look, he added, "oh, you just want us to leave the room."

Issy tapped her nose and winked at him.

"Fine. Gibbs, let's go." The two stood and made their way down the hallway to the kitchen.

Patchwork had gone straight to his room upon returning home. He had seemed excited to go on the mission, but the violence and the threat against his life seemed to have removed all his vigor. He had simply told them that he needed some time to himself, and Moss figured he was in his room, hiding in the Mass Illusion.

"So," Moss said as they entered the kitchen. "How was it, really?"

Gibbs let out a long sigh. He looked tired and not full of life as Moss had hoped and expected he would after getting back from his honeymoon.

"The place was amazing, getting away was amazing, getting to spend time together was amazing, but, as always seems to happen, shit hit the fan too."

"Oh?" was all Moss needed to say. He knew his friend would keep talking.

"Ynna begged me not to say anything," Gibbs said, his eyes flashing down the hall as though she could hear them. "I, it was actually more like, she threatened my life if I said anything."

"So don't say anything," Moss said with a smile, before adding theatrically, "and I'll just wonder for our whole lives what you didn't tell me and you'll know that, because of it, our lives were just that little bit worse."

Gibbs rolled his eyes. "You know I want to tell you, and really you know I'm going to," he said with a sad chuckle. "We … ran into an old friend of Ynna's … and it was ugly. Changed the whole trip."

Moss wanted to ask so much more. He was always so interested in Ynna's history, but he didn't want to push his friend. "I see," was all he said. "I'm really sorry."

"Me too," Gibbs said sadly. "We really needed this. She really needed this. This whole thing is so relentless and, despite everything between them, Sandra was like a mother to Ynna after she lost her own. She won't admit, or can't admit, how much this loss has devastated her, but I can see it."

"She's lost so many people that she sometimes closes herself off entirely, but I can see it too," Moss said. "with everyone, really."

"Yeah," Gibbs said and a put a hand on his friend's shoulder. "How are you doing?"

"I'm … okay …"

Gibbs frowned. "You know you can't bullshit me."

"I'm all kinds of fucked," Moss told him frankly and it felt good to let the words out. "My grandmother is dead, Issy was shot, Judy has run off … it just feels like everything is in turmoil. We've had such great successes and people are looking to us to change the world, but it feels like the world is coming apart at the seams. This team is my family now, but it's one hell of a dysfunctional family and I don't know how to keep us all together."

"It's not your job to," Gibbs said soothingly.

"But it should be. I'm supposed to be a leader."

"Well, real leadership is different than it is in the movies," Gibbs said with a smile. "It's not about command presence, always knowing what to do, or always making the right decisions. Real-life leadership is about reacting to tough situations, getting out in front of things when you can and turning to your team when you need help. Or, in this case, your family when you need help."

Moss nodded; his friend was right. "Thanks, man."

Gibbs studied his face. "But that's not all."

"What do you mean?"

"There's something else, something you're not telling me," Gibbs said.

Moss chuckled quietly. "Who even are you? What happened to the guy who just quoted movies all the time and didn't seem to have an ounce of depth?"

"Pretty sure you got that guy killed," Gibbs said with a laugh. "And anyway, I'm trying to cut back on the quotes – I told you that Ynna doesn't like them."

"Issy and I complained about them for years, but it never stopped you before," Moss said with a wink.

"Well, you guys put out less than she does," Gibbs said with a smirk.

Moss laughed as he walked over to the fridge and grabbed a couple beers. "Okay, let's get these back." But as he walked towards the door, Gibbs put a hand on his chest.

"Not until you tell me."

Moss sighed. "Noticed that, did you?"

"Seriously, man, I'm not the kid you left the burbs with, and you're not that naïve dumbfuck whose biggest problem was a fellow engineer being mean to you. If you're this worried, something is really going on. So, tell me."

Moss nodded. "It's the program."

"It always is. What is it now?"

"It's fritzing something fierce," Moss admitted. "Like, it's somehow pounding on my brain so badly that it's knocking me out of chairs and shit. It's scary. No, it's terrifying. My own mind is corrupted, and I don't know what that means for my present or my future, but I know it's not good."

"What you doing about it?"

"Upping the dampeners and hoping it passes, keeping an eye on it ..." it sounded like a dumb answer even to himself.

Gibbs considered that for a moment and then said, "Have you considered going in?"

Moss shook his head. "No, there's too much risk. If I come off the dampeners, who knows what would happen?"

"Right, who knows?" Gibbs said, shaking his head. "But I'm not sure it could be any worse than getting knocked out of a chair by your own brain. What will happen if it crops up during a firefight or while we're out on some dangerous mission? Something like this could get you killed — if it doesn't straight up kill you itself. Or it could get one of us killed ... like Issy ..."

"You've got a point," Moss had to admit, although he didn't want to consider the possibility of going back into the program now. There were so many other moving parts and the idea of reopening this Pandora's box seemed like an unnecessary risk. "Patchwork says that if it knocks me unconscious, he's going to uninstall it."

129

"I'm with him on that," Gibbs said. "I know you think we need it, but we've been making do without it."

The beers were making his hand cold and he set all but one down, cracking the cap and taking a swig before answering, "It's not just that I think we need it, it's like I know we need it. There's something telling me that before the end, it's going to be required for victory."

Gibbs walked over and cracked one of the beers himself, taking such a large gulp that half the beer was gone when he set the bottle down. "Don't give me that fatalistic bullshit. Even you don't believe it. You just don't want to lose your dad."

That one hurt. Not only because there was an element of truth to it, but also because of the element of untruth. For reasons that he couldn't explain, he genuinely did believe that this program was going to be necessary. He didn't know how or why, but he knew he couldn't let it go. Not until after ThutoCo was destroyed.

"Look, man, I'm not gonna lie and say that the dad part isn't a factor. It is but believe me when I say that there's more to it."

Gibbs seemed to recognize the sincerity in his voice. "Okay, but I'm going to be keeping an eye on you."

"Fine," Moss said, knowing that his friend was just coming from a place of caring. "I really do appreciate it."

"Good," Gibbs said, "and remember, we actually are getting close."

"Close to what?"

"The end. Of all this."

Moss laughed. "I got news for you; this never ends. I have started to think about what comes next. It's even more of a clusterfuck than this."

Taking another sip that polished off the bottle, Gibbs's face changed into a clever little smirk. "Awesome, wow. Do you have a clue what happens now?"

"Exactly," Moss said, knowing a reference for once. "Even if we somehow purge the planets of the megas, we still have to figure out what the hell to do."

"Sure," Gibbs relented. "That's one way of looking at it. The next part will be impossible and the next, on and on ad infinitum, but," and he said the 'but' with exaggerated flourish, "you could also look at defeating the megas as what it would be — a victory. *The* victory."

"Wasn't it you who literally just told me that things don't always look as clean as they do in the movies?" Moss said incredulously.

Gibbs smiled, pointed and winked at Moss, and for a moment it felt like they were back in Moss's hex. "Yes, but this is different. Of course, every new beginning comes from some other beginning's end, but it is also an end. If you win The Cup, you can relish your victory before looking to the next season."

Moss let a crooked little smile cross his lips. "I'll admit, relaxing on a beach always looked pretty great."

That made Gibbs grin from ear to ear, and he clapped Moss on the shoulder. "There you go!"

They smiled at each other a moment before Moss asked something that he had been wondering about. "What will you do afterward?"

"If we beat the megas?"

"Yeah," Moss said. "If we win The Cup this season, what will you do afterward?"

Gibbs looked off wistfully, lost in some dream for a moment, and said, "I'm the third of my name. I suppose there should be a fourth."

"Feels like we were just kids ourselves," Moss observed.

"The way we lived kept us children for a lot longer," Gibbs noted. "I'm honestly not sure that anybody in the burbs ever really grows up. Being sheltered like that, never leaving, you may as well just be in the womb your whole life."

"Ynna really is rubbing off on you."

"Good," Gibbs said. "But really, being married, doing this whole traditional-ass thing, kind of makes me want to be traditional."

"I can appreciate that," Moss said. "There has to be more to this life."

"I think that was really the difference between them," Gibbs led.

"Between who?"

"Between Sandra and Burn," Gibbs said, and for the first time in a while, Moss felt the punch in his brain. His head rocketed backward and he fell into the refrigerator.

"Holy shit!" Gibbs exclaimed and rushed over to help. Footsteps came crashing down the hallway and seconds later the girls joined them in the room.

"That program again?" Issy asked in mingled anger and terror as she rushed to Moss's side.

Moss blinked hard, letting Issy help him into one of the chairs at the kitchen table. Knowing he shouldn't, he took another swig of his beer and turned to Ynna. "You know what I could really use?"

Shaking her head, Ynna smiled and produced a pack of cigarettes, pulling one out and handing it to Moss. She didn't bother offering one to Issy or Gibbs.

132

"Telling me about it was one thing," Gibbs said in a shaky voice. "But seeing it for myself, I think I agree with Patchwork. We should just get that thing out of your brain."

"Maybe you're right," Moss said as he put the cigarette in his mouth and Ynna flicked the lighter.

Moss felt the heat. But something wasn't right. The heat was too intense and his body was being propelled backwards. He heard crashing sounds, felt himself smashing through a wall. His lungs burned. He saw fire, smoke and debris. There were screams. His head rang and he didn't understand what was happening.

He turned his head as if in slow motion. Flames licked all around him. There was nothing but fire. He was on the ground but hadn't registered getting there. It was a blur. His whole life was a blur. He saw Issy, his beautiful love, running along the crumbling floor, firing a pistol.

He saw armor. White armor with gray. He knew that armor.

Then it all clicked.

Zetas.

ThutoCo had found them. It had only been a matter of time. And they weren't messing around now. A Zeta pointed at him then another pointed a weapon. He felt his body lurch again. He was being pulled. He tried to turn to look but the flames just streaked his vision. He was gone.

CHAPTER 14

Moss felt his eyes open and saw green. He darted upright, a strange smell filling his nose. The burning was gone, replaced by wet earth and a smell he couldn't identify — almost like the smell of the fresh air.

He moved his hands to the ground, feeling them sink into dirt. It was a strange sensation, an unfamiliar one. His was a world of glass and plastic, cement and metal. He blinked up at the sky, watching as a few leaves danced down toward him from the canopy.

He didn't understand. How was he so far from the city? As he took in another breath, fear gripped him before he remembered that everything he had been told about the outside world was a lie. He could breathe here and not be infected by the spores.

He stood. His body didn't hurt. He didn't feel any of the scorch marks he had expected. Taking a step forward, he felt the grass and leaves between his toes and under the pads of his feet. It felt wonderful and he looked down to see that he was nude.

Trees soared into the sky and he could only hear the sound of leaves in the wind. Until he heard a faint babbling sound in the distance. He followed it instinctually, as though he was floating toward it. He didn't know why, but he wanted to go that way. His breath steamed white clouds but his body didn't feel cold. The sun on the horizon peeked through the tree line either rising or setting, but Moss didn't know which.

He crested a little rise and saw a stream at the bottom of a little gully. Across from it was a steep wall. He saw two creatures moving in the distance. He moved closer, not feeling the need to hide or creep; he simply strode toward the shapes. One was small and brown, and his heart soared as he saw the cub. The little bear was cute, but Moss knew it was still dangerous. He had seen bears once before as his family drove toward Carcer City long ago, and remembered the pure awe he had felt. The little animal took no notice of Moss as it scampered along the ridge of the rise.

He followed as it moved toward the other shape. Moss understood that the larger animal was a shadow of what it had once been. The older bear moved slowly, its clawed feet padding heavily along the ridge. Gray streaked its fur and ribs showed through on its side. It was an ancient animal, but Moss knew it could still rip him to smithereens if given the chance.

Seeing these animals made Moss happier than he could remember being. Simply standing out in the wild, away from people and the shit they made, was something he wanted to feel all the time. In this moment, watching the two animals move along the ridge above, he realized that *this* was what he wanted for the planet, what he had always wanted. He had picked up the mantle from his family, but it was the natural world that truly inspired him. In whatever new world they created if they won their fight, he wanted to make sure there was a place for these animals. Thinking of his conversation with Gil, he realized that he wanted more than just a few safe spaces for them amid the ubiquity of man.

A growl distracted him from his thoughts. The little bear was calling out at some enemy, some distant threat blocked from Moss's sight by the ridge. The ancient bear let out a roar that shook the ground, terrified birds from the trees and seemed to rattle Moss's ribs. The little bear moved under the big one, staying between its legs and making little yipping sounds.

The big bear reared up and bellowed again, and Moss watched in horror as its right hind leg slipped in the wet earth. Before he could do anything the animal plummeted off the ridge. He ran forward, arms pumping as he moved. He could hear shallow breaths as he skidded in the loose rocks along the river's bank. He looked down into those old eyes staring up at him, — or was it beyond him? Craning its neck, the bear looked up at the cub with an expression of guilt. Moss understood, but as he turned back, he heard a roar and lifted his hands in defense.

But it was too late. The adult male came out of nowhere, rushing toward Moss with teeth bared, and he clamped his eyes closed.

Air blasted from his lungs and everything hurt. He opened his eyes to the rain, feeling metal jamming into his back. He looked around and saw the neon lights of home. Or of the city. He tried to move but his body seemed unwilling to answer him.

"Get a job," a man snarled from under an umbrella as he walked by, having to step over Moss. Then he heard the man say into his call, "This fucking city."

Moss tried to communicate, call out to Seti, to anyone, but he felt static in his mind. It was as if there was a layer of mold on his brain. He could see the singe marks on his clothes and smelled blood and burning through the rain. Though his whole body ached, he managed to force himself up and look around. He'd been lying on the sidewalk in a part of the city he did not recognize, its endless streets with endless shops serving the faceless millions.

He reached around to tap the emergency release of the dronepack on his back. It had been jamming into his spine. Someone must have put it on him and activated it back in the safe house, sending him rocketing to safety, away from the ThutoCo attack. He reached out again, trying to communicate with someone. He hoped they were okay, needed them to be okay. He took solace in the thought that if anyone could survive an attack like this, it would be his crew, his family.

Though they were cybernetic, his legs were so attuned to his brain that they shook with tension and fear as he began walking down the street. He needed to figure out how to get home — or rather, where home even was now.

"An emergency, or if we all get separated," Seti had always told them, "just call me."

He laughed to himself. Their reliance on technology had come back to bite them. He couldn't call Seti, couldn't call anyone, and now he didn't know what to do. He staggered forward under an awning to get out of the rain. Looking up and down the street, he saw neon lights pointing down a staircase. A bar.

He lurched forward, leaning against a car before pushing himself across the street, nearly getting run over by a rickshaw as the driver hollered something at him. He kept moving, grabbing the handrail as he nearly fell down the stairs. The rain was so heavy that he could not tell if he was leaving blood in the street; but looking down, he he saw no open wounds. Just scorched clothes.

Elbowing the metal door open, Moss didn't even look around. He just made his way to the nearest bar stool and flopped down beside an old man who looked like a tanned raisin in coveralls. He panted with exertion and the water flowed off his body to pool under the stool. He wondered how long he had been out in the street, how long people had walked over him and left him there. As he had been dreaming of the wildlife he wanted to save, the humanity he was saving had left him to die.

"Jack on ice and a dreamscape," the old man ordered, turning to Moss and saying, "on me." The bartender hobbled away, a crutch made of PVC pipe keeping him upright as one pant leg dangled empty.

"Thank you," Moss croaked, surprised that his voice even worked.

"My pleasure," the man said, holding out a hand. "Sam's the name."

"Moss," Moss said hoarsely. He would normally use a nom de plume but he was too exhausted to care.

"Moss, let me tell you a story," the man began and continued talking without skipping a beat. "When I was a boy, we lived in one of those jumbo buildings, you know the ones? Sure you do. Well, I lived in one of them. The man below us was a digihead, or at least that's what my dad called them at the time, but I'm sure you know the type – the ones you don't unplug.

"Anyway, he was one of them types and he spent his whole life on the virtual. Worse now, but bad then too. Maurice, I want to say his name was, but that's not particularly relevant. Spent his time in the virtual and it was before the days of them biofeeders like we have now. So, once a day, Maurice had to unplug to feed himself and take a shit. Well, he unplugged and made his way to the kitchen to cook what we later learned was a pack mac & cheese. Started cooking, went to the bathroom and then went right back into the digital. In all the years since, I've wondered whether he forgot about the food or thought he would just pop into the virtual and pop right back out but as you'll hear in a second, I'll never find out.

"Maurice ... I swear his name was Maurice ... well, it may have been Morris ... he didn't remember to come back out, as so many don't, but his stovetop didn't have the auto shutoff link to his gaming rig like they do now, so his apartment went up. Course nowadays, the place would be bricked with foam, but back then he just roasted like a stuck pig; cooking alive as his mind danced the cha-cha or whatever escape he had picked.

"A few days later, friends and me broke into his place at night. Normal kids' shit, thinking we were tough for going to a place where a dead body had been. But we opened that door and we smelt it: that stink of a man baked right into his chair. Smell got in my nose and lasted for weeks. Couldn't hardly close my eyes without sucking in that man's death. Ugly stuff that."

He stopped speaking for a moment and Moss just stared at him with his mouth agape, having no idea where he was going with all this. The bartender set the drink down along with a small plate bearing a pill.

"Thanks," Moss said and turned back to Sam.

The old man's face wrinkled as he grinned and said, "You smell like that."

Moss burst out laughing. It was a sound that blasted out from somewhere deep within him, as though all the absurdities of the miserable world needed a release.

"I'm sure I do," Moss said through the laughter, tears beginning to stream down his face.

His home was gone. He had no idea where his friends were or if they were okay. They had been found and were once again on their heels. The laughter just kept coming with the tears. He began to cough, tasting blood.

"You all right, there, friend?" Sam asked, a look of genuine concern pulling his brows together.

Moss kept laughing, wiping his cheek with hands stained black with soot, now running with moisture.

"No," he said, putting the drink to his lips and sucking it down. "I'm so far from okay."

"And that's okay, too," Sam said with a grin.

Moss stopped, sniffled and looked at the man. "Yes," Moss said. "Thank you."

"Sometimes we need to be reminded of that," Sam said. "Feel like the weight o' the world is on our shoulders but we ain't Atlas, you know. We are just us. We can do what we can do."

Moss smiled. "Right, that's all we can do."

"Anything else I can do for you, friend?" Sam asked and the sincerity of the man continued to amaze Moss. This old stranger, this strange old man, showed nothing but kindness.

"No," Moss said with a smile. All the laughter had hurt and now he was swimming in a sea of pain, but looking at the dreamscape, he couldn't convince himself to get high. It wasn't the right time. He needed to find his friends. "Actually, can you tell me where we are?"

The man looked around the room, the dingy bar with its few televisions and quiet patrons, and said, "This here's a bar."

"The neighborhood, I mean."

"Oh," the man said with a wry smile. "Ninth and Irving."

"Oh!" Moss exclaimed. "I'm just across the park from home."

"One of *those* nights, eh?"

"Something like that." Moss stood too quickly in his excitement. Pain raged through him and he nearly collapsed, having to grip the bar to keep himself upright. He grabbed the dreamscape and tucked it in his pocket. "Never know when you need this."

"Got that right," Sam said, winking a wrinkled eye.

As Moss turned to leave, the booze started to help little bit. He turned back to Sam and said, "Before I go, is there anything I can do for you?"

Sam looked at him pensively and answered, "Can you kill my ex-wife?"

Moss shook his head. "Way to ruin the mood, Sam. But it was nice meeting you."

"And you, Mulch."

Chuckling, Moss ascended the stairs, and looked at the street with new eyes. He'd been here countless times, but blasted and concussed, it looked like a foreign world. He began making his way towards the park. Though it was closed at night (otherwise it would have become a tent-city generations earlier), there were guarded walking paths that allowed people passage.

Moss wished he had had a second drink to ease a bit more of the pain, but he was beginning to move a little bit more naturally. He knew he would have to be looked at, but he figured that he wasn't mortally wounded. As he walked past an alleyway, he turned his head briefly to see a man yanking on a leash. The dog at the end yelped and the man yelled at the animal.

Moss's body turned before he even realized what was happening, his eyes fixated on the dog. The man muttered something again, before swinging a foot. The dog cried out as it was kicked in the side and then gargled when its neck caught in the collar.

"What the fuck are you doing?" Moss growled as he approached the man, his words reverberating off the wall.

"How I deal with my dog is my business," the man said before even turning around; but when he did, he looked Moss over and seemed to deem him a homeless person, and not worth his time. "Get away from me, bum."

The dog squeaked one more time and that was all it took. Everything, all the rage Moss felt towards a world that was unfair to too many people, to himself and everyone he loved, came out of him in one moment. He struck the man with a force with which he had never hit anybody.. The man landed on the ground with a crash, and Moss could tell one of his wrists broke on impact.

The leash had fallen out of his hands andthe dog took off in the direction of freedom. The man stood.

"What the fuck, you crazy!" he shrieked in pain, anger and fear. He held up his hands as though he was going to try to fight Moss, but one of them fell limp.

"How could you do that?" Moss said, genuinely unable to understand how a person could hurt an animal in that way.

"It's just a dog, and more to the point, it's my fucking dog," the man announced as though that was the answer to everything.

The next hit broke his nose and sent him staggering back. Blood streamed down his face in the rain and he looked at Moss in utter confusion. Moss moved in closer, looming over the man.

"It's just a fucking animal," he whimpered and that was it.

Moss grabbed his collar and began to punch. Once, twice, again and again and again. Blood sprayed and the man went limp. Must beat the world, the people who had stolen his parents from him, the people who killed Stan, Rosetta, Anders and everyone else he loved. He beat the world for not caring, for its apathy. And he beat this man for everything else. And for the dog.

When he let go and the man's body slumped into the street, Moss no longer felt anything. He knew what he had become. He had been forced to become this thing. It was just like Gibbs had said: things weren't clean, binary. To become a hero, Moss had been forced to perform acts of villainy. His grandmother had tried to keep him from becoming that person, but he had just the same. Burn had tried to convince him that any corporate goon needed to die because they would kill if you didn't kill them first, but that had largely just been an excuse, a way to justify the means.

Looking at his reflection in the puddle beside the body, Moss didn't really know what he was anymore.

"Moss?"

He turned to see Issy, Gibbs, Patchwork and Ynna.

CHAPTER 15

"If he's doing that to a dog, who knows what he's doing to other people," Issy offered by way of justification, though it sounded more like it was for herself than for him.

Ynna rolled her eyes. "Another fucking abusive scumbag being left dead in the street isn't even worth concerning ourselves with."

"How did you even find me?" Moss asked as Gibbs walked over to the table with a bottle and five glasses.

"Shit, how hard did you hit your head?" Ynna asked with a laugh. "We tracked the dronepack, of course."

"Right," Moss said as he looked around the table and his friends. They were all in rough shape, their clothes burned, their hair wet and their bloodied faces dark. But they were alive and that's all that mattered. Gibbs poured the alcohol and everyone began to drink immediately. Sam looked over from his spot from the bar and gave a nearly imperceptible nod, and Moss raised his glass in a bloodied hand of bruised knuckles.

"What now?"

"Tak is coming to meet us here and get us set up with a new place," Patchwork told them.

"Good," Moss said. "We'll need some time to rest before we move on D2E the second Rude contacts us."

"Are you fucking kidding me?" Ynna said, disgust dripping off every word. "We're not going to some new fucking hideout to lick our wounds. We are going to get geared up now and make ThutoCo pay for this!"

"Hon," Gibbs began but Ynna held up a hand.

"For a start, don't ever 'hon' me in this kind of context you fucking bub and second, ThutoCo just destroyed our home and nearly killed us. We are not going back underground; we've come too far for that. We own this city. We got Carcer out and somehow we're still getting shot at every other day. Nope. No way. Nuh uh. We will have Tak set us up with some weapons and Seti give us a spot to fuck up."

"Puck beat the snot out of Arthur Smith," Gibbs noted. "That's something."

"That ain't shit," Ynna snapped. "It's time these assholes took us seriously. We'll get Seti to give us a target and were going tonight." She narrowed her eyes at Moss and added, "*We* haven't all been able to paint the pavement with our rage yet."

She had a point. As much as he didn't like to admit it, he had found an outlet for his anger. "I suppose it's not like ThutoCo doesn't deserve it."

"All that to say you agree with me?" Ynna said.

Moss let out a long sigh. "D2E is our primary target at the moment but ThutoCo won't stop until we are all dead, so if you guys want some good old-fashioned revenge, I'm fine with it."

"I'm happy we have your permission, my liege," Ynna scoffed.

"It isn't like that," Moss said, "and you know it."

Gibbs stepped in to defuse the moment. "I'm happy to fuck up my old employer."

"Me too," Issy said quietly.

"How did they find us?" Patchwork asked. He didn't appear to have been listening and all eyes turned to him. "You think Judy ratted us out?"

That changed the tone at the table in an instant. "What?" Moss asked at the same time that Ynna barked it.

"I mean, they stormed out of the room and then we were hit almost immediately," he said. "The timing is suspicious."

"Coincidental," Ynna corrected with an outstretched finger. "Some of us have shorter fuses or struggle to keep our shit in check. Doesn't make us fucking finks. Even Moss just dropped some fucking rando. Think he's going to rat?" she added for good measure.

Moss hated the way his actions were being discussed, but he supposed that was the way it had to be. He had his own complicated feelings on what had happened. He didn't even feel like himself and it made him question himself.

"It's not that, I'm simply —" Patch was cutoff.

"Could have just as easily been Tak," Ynna added accusingly.

Patchwork's mouth fell open. "It wasn't Tak!"

"You know that just as much as I know Judy didn't. Only difference is you are fucking one of them and don't want it to be true!" Ynna was nearly shouting now.

"How about it wasn't either of us!" Judy snapped and all heads turned to see them and Tak standing side by side at the bar. They both looked quite well put-together compared to the scorched and bullet-riddled rest of the crew.

"That was actually the point I was trying to make," Ynna justified.

"Whatever," Judy said and slid into the booth, snatching the bottle and taking a swig. Tak moved in beside Patchwork and kissed him on the cheek.

"Where were you?" Patchwork made a show of asking Judy.

"Not that it's any of your fucking business, but I had to get out of there," they said coldly. "Stan and I fell in love around The Holiday and seeing that store brought up some shit for me. And I'm sitting at a table with three happy couples and my lover is in some Carcer mass grave, so forgive me if I've got some feelings that need to breathe."

Patchwork's face flushed and he dropped his head. "Sorry, Judy, you're right."

"No shit," Judy snapped.

Moss turned to them and said, "I'm happy you're back," and then added to Tak, "Good to see you again."

"Y- you too," he muttered, clearly intimidated by the company. His eyes kept flashing at Ynna. Moss understood the reputation of the woman: she was a badass and everyone knew it.

"How did you find us?" Moss asked, his mind still in a fog. Everyone looked at him like he was an idiot.

"Seti told us," Tak said in nearly a whisper.

"Ah," Moss said. "My link is disrupted. One more thing for the list."

"The new place I got you will have supplies for that," Tak said, a little smile crossing his lips.

"Yeah?" Moss asked, by way of allowing the young man to brag.

"Yep," he said. "The new spot is even more hidden and has much better supplies. Without Carcer breathing down our necks, I was able to set up something pretty badass."

"Sounds like we should have moved sooner," Issy said with a little smile. Moss could tell her mind was elsewhere. The image of him over that man had upset her badly.

Tak looked at them, a half-guilty expression crossing his face. He was dressed for his job, as he seemed to be whenever Moss had seen him. He wore cargo pants with pockets filled to bursting, a vest with tools hanging from every inch, and external implants on both temples that projected a digital display before his eyes. Cable ties hung from his belt and the hands that gripped the recently-filled glass were rough and callused.

"Sandra told me that she didn't want you guys to move."

Everyone looked at him in shock before their faces contorted as they tried to figure out why Sandra had made that decision. Everyone had seen the woman so differently and they all seemed to be working out their own version of her thinking.

"Why?"

Tak laughed and looked at Moss incredulously. "You think she told me anything?"

Now Moss felt left out, too. "No, I suppose she wouldn't have."

"I was ... I was sorry to hear about her," Tak said looking at Moss and then averting his eyes.

Moss took a swig of his drink and replied quietly, "Thank you." He didn't know Tak well at all, but so far was happy to have him there.

"So, do you guys want to see the place?" Tak asked.

Everybody looked at Ynna. She shook her head. "No, we want you to take us to the closest available weapons and then we are gonna fuck up ThutoCo."

"Oh," Tak said in surprise. "What are you going to hit? It'll help me figure out what weapons to get."

Nobody spoke for a long moment, then, very quietly, Issy put in, "I know a place."

"You do?" several of them said in unison.

"Yeah, I mean I *was* BurbSec …" she said in nearly a whisper. Moss couldn't believe what he was hearing. She had discussed this with him but he never thought she would mention it.

"So?" Ynna asked, trying to sound casual, but there was an unmistakable urgency in the word.

"So …" Issy said, clearly still struggling with this decision. "I've seen a part of the facility where I believe they train the Alphas."

"What the fuck, Is?" Ynna exclaimed. "How have you not told us this before?"

"Because, while I may hate ThutoCo now, I was BurbSec and the idea of killing a whole bunch of people who are basically me doesn't really sit well with me. Sorry if that pisses you off, but we all have to grapple with the morality of what we're doing and how we do it."

Issy didn't break eye contact and Ynna nodded slowly. "I understand," she said in such a way so that nobody doubted her sincerity. "We can do this in a way that respects that. There's no reason that we have to go in and hurt a bunch of Podunk police from the burbs."

"Oh," Issy said, genuinely surprised. "Thank you."

"I'm not Sandra," Ynna said, "nor is Moss his grandmother. We can do these things, and we can do them right. We can go back to feeling like Robin Hood. Despite what we just saw, and in spite of what we all know I've done, this is not a vendetta."

"It's true," Moss agreed. "We can do this right. And listen," he said, his eyes downcast. "You all know I've been struggling. You all know that Sandra's death has kinda fucked me up, but after now, after this, it's all out of my system. I'll be better now."

He meant it sincerely but wasn't sure how true it was. He wanted to be better, have a better grip on himself, but he knew that something had changed. Looking up, he saw cautious optimism on everyone's faces. Except Issy's. She knew him too well. And while Gibbs might fall for it, she would not.

"We're all struggling," Judy sympathized. "There is more pain at this table than nearly any place in the city ... and this city has *a lot* of pain. It manifests in all of us differently, but being here for each other is what defines us. You guys have stuck with me through everything and I'll stick with all of you to the bitter end. We will put a dent in ThutoCo today, drop the hammer on D2E tomorrow, and who the hell knows? Maybe we'll take down the whole fucking AIC next week, next month or next year. But we'll do it together. As a team. As a family."

"Hear hear," Moss said, raising his glass.

They all raised their glasses, clinking them together. What Judy had said was true. Everyone at this table was always carrying a huge amount of emotional weight. They all had been hurt so deeply and lost so much. But that which could have divided others united them. It made them stronger and they found solace in each other they would never have found elsewhere. It was a remarkable thing.

As he gulped down his drink, Moss wouldn't have wanted to be anywhere else, with anyone else.

CHAPTER 16

Moss's eyes flashed between the screen and the endless containers before him. He tried to remember where they had turned, what rows they had ducked into.

They crouched along the road waiting for their opportunity. Several trucks had left the facility, but none had been the ones they were seeking. They had been waiting a very long time and everyone was antsy. After having gone to grab weapons, they were raring to go; but now they had to wait, pressed along the walls of an alleyway outside a nondescript building.

Another one coming, Gibbs let them know from his elevated position.

Scanning now, Patchwork relayed. He had once again repaired Moss's neural mesh so that he was able to hear and communicate, but Moss could tell that everything with his program was really starting to bother his friend. He knew it was starting to bother all of them, and even he was getting tired of himself and the chip in his head.

Got a hit.

Nobody answered, but as they saw the truck bouncing forward, Issy stepped into the street in her BurbSec armor. She had gone back to the old safe house while they were gathering their weapons to find it. It had been in a metal footlocker and while it had taken significant damage, just enough was left that she could wear it. In fact, the scarring and scorch marks actually helped to sell the lie.

"Oh, thank you so much for stopping," she gasped at the truck driver as he pulled to a stop. She yanked the helmet from her head and shook her hair free. The driver's side door opened, and the driver pulled himself up and halfway out to shout to Issy as she jogged over.

"What the hell happened to you?" he asked, fear in his voice. BurbSec officers were not particularly tough, but those that took the driver role, navigating supplies through the city, had to at least be somewhat savvy and prepared for battle.

Issy approached the driver. "I was heading to work, and I know we're supposed to change on site, but you know how it is when you're running late and you just need to get to your shift on time, and I was jumped. These guys came out of nowhere and just started beating me, shouting about the new revolution, and get the megas out of B.A. City. I was so scared."

The driver cocked his head and his body tightened as she neared the door. Moss didn't think he was buying it and he gripped his Kingfisher, ready to move at a moment's notice.

"Sorry, friend, but I gotta tell you this doesn't add up," crackled from the driver's side and he began to close his door. But Issy was too close, too smart and too fast. She had her weapon loosed in a flash and hit the passenger with a bolt between the armor plates.

The door struck her shoulder as the driver slammed it into her and Moss begin to move. He couldn't stand to see her hurt again. He raised his weapon as he ran, but Issy had already sent hers crashing into the man's head. He was dazed but not down and he tried to slam her with the door again, but this time she pressed the barrel of her weapon between the plates at his neck and fired.

By the time Moss had a clear shot, both BurbSec officers were already down. "Are you okay?" Moss asked as he skidded to a stop beside Issy.

She turned and smiled at him. "Yeah, I'm fine. This armor can take more than a car door." She pulled the driver's glove off and Patchwork got to work immediately, hacking the embedded operator's chip.

They all looked around impatiently, waiting for somebody to call out from a window or for a car to pass, but it remained quiet. They had picked the spot for this very reason. Being between warehouses was good cover for the Academy but being in an industrial zone also worked in their favor as it meant the streets were empty at this time of night.

"Got it," Patchwork said with a grin and handed the glove to Issy. She put it on and rushed around towards the back of the van as Patchwork concluded, "Shit, I'm good."

Everyone followed Issy as Patch looked at them expectantly. Gibbs finally relented, saying, "You really are."

"I know, thank you!"

They all giggled as Issy swung the door open, revealing the armor and supplies. Everyone began piling in as Issy returned to the front, pushing the driver to the side and taking his spot. Using his glove, she took control of the van and began driving slowly into an alleyway. In the back, with much difficulty, everyone began to undress as Issy drove. Feet slid and armor clattered as they dressed as quickly as they could in the swaying vehicle.

Issy spun the van to face toward the street and killed the lights before stopping. She looked back at everybody and asked, "What are we doing with these two?"

Without saying a word, Ynna tossed a small bag through the little opening to the cab. Issy caught it and pulled out handcuffs and red ball gags on leather straps. "Are these … from your personal collection?"

"Wanna find out?" Ynna said with a wink and Gibbs flushed a bright shade of crimson. Once Patchwork was dressed in the armor, he reopened the back doors and hopped out to place small holoprojectors next to the license plates to display the new numbers. Meanwhile, Issy scrolled through the display in front of the driver's seat to create a new manifest that matched the new license plate number.

Once their cover was in place, they were back on the road and headed towards the Academy. Sitting in the back in BurbSec armor, Moss smiled at everybody and said, "Odysseus would be proud."

"Ooh, we're so impressed that you read the book everybody on earth is forced to read in school," Ynna said in mocking tone and pulled the BurbSec helmet over her pink hair.

"Do you always have to bust my balls?" Moss sighed as he pulled his own helmet over his head.

He could hear the smile he couldn't see when Ynna responded, "Yes. Yes, I do."

As they pulled up to the nondescript warehouse, they were stopped at a gatehouse in front of a rolling iron gate. Tire spikes stuck out from the ground. The woman within made a show of groaning out of her seat to look at her computer console. She was dressed in the tight Blacks of a small security firm that undoubtedly didn't exist. She was a BurbSec officer but couldn't appear to be one without giving away the façade that this was not just some shipping warehouse.

Moss thought it was perfect corporate idiocy to believe that nobody would notice that all the trucks going into and coming out of this facility were driven by people dressed in full BurbSec armor.

Without saying a word, the woman found their truck on the doctored document and pressed the button to open the gate, waving them through before sitting down and plucking a book off her little desk. Moss noticed the small paper thing, as his grandmother was one of few people he had ever seen reading proper printed books. Every now and again he would grab one and leaf through it, but he found the words printed on paper difficult to read.

The van continued toward the warehouse and was quickly scanned as a it pulled up to another rolling gate. They stopped for only a second before the gate opened, revealing a shabby old auto repair shop. Moss was surprised as he gazed out through the windshield, but as Issy pulled forward and passed through the projected image, he was no longer surprised. The gate rolled closed behind them as they pulled forward into a state-of-the-art BurbSec facility.

A fully kitted-out officer waiting just inside pointed their van toward a row of equally nondescript parked vans. The room was all white, illuminated by fluorescent lights dangling from the ceiling. The BurbSec logo was painted everywhere and there were digital displays around the room showing cadets, potential recruits and other proprietary ThutoCo information.

Even though Moss had seen so much and been through so much, there was something about seeing behind the scenes of the company for which he used to work that made him feel guilty. He felt like a child who had been left unattended somewhere he shouldn't be; but he shook his head and laughed at the absurdity of the feeling.

Issy hopped out after parking and Moss simultaneously opened the back doors of the van. The officer who had guided them in came over in his white plate over black mesh armor and said, "Here for upgrades?"

Moss had happened to grab the armor of a BurbSec manager, so he answered, "Yes, we are moving up in the world."

The man shot them a thumbs up. "Congratulations. With Carcer gone, we need Zetas more than ever."

"You can say that again," Moss said with a laugh. "Where we heading?"

The man gestured in the direction of an unmarked staircase leading down and Moss began heading that direction.

Don't walk so fast, Patchwork communicated. *They have a lot of protection and it's going to take me a while to break everything.*

Copy, Moss said as they descended the stairs. Moss had expected them to lead to a labyrinthine set of tunnels, but instead the staircase opened into a wide space decorated with plants under vitamin D lights. There were statues and screens and benches and everything you could want to take a little rest between training sessions. Signs clearly pointed in different directions, letting new recruits know exactly where they needed to go.

"Holy shit," Judy remarked aloud under their breath. "ThutoCo really doesn't mess around when it comes to amenities."

"Carcer didn't do things this way?" Moss asked as they walked past a burbling water feature.

"You've been inside a Carcer facility," Judy scoffed. "It's as much a prison for the staff as for anybody else. They spend as little as they can and then just hang posters about productivity everywhere."

A recruit filling a cup at a fancy drink dispenser gave a little wave and the crew awkwardly waved back. Issy said, "Well, that's how they get you. ThutoCo wasn't built on evil schemes alone, and you're happy to be a sheep."

"Makes sense," Judy said. "Cows who like their pasture are probably less likely to cause a stink."

"Pretty sure a cow is always liable to cause a stink," Gibbs joked, and no one laughed.

"Ouch," Ynna mocked.

Moss chuckled. "Yeah, man, not your best work."

To the left, here, Patchwork told them. *That unmarked door.*

They turned and made their way toward the door like a flock of birds and Moss felt the familiar throb of anticipation in his heart. This next part would not be easy. They had been lucky to make short work of simply getting into the facility but dealing with the Zetas would be different. He became hyperaware of the fact that he was carrying small explosive devices under his armor.

Moss took the lead and headed toward a door with a little squiggle over it. *Go for it,* Patchwork said, and Moss waved his glove over the keypad. It honked and a red light flashed. Moss thought maybe the breaking hadn't worked and that in a moment all eyes would be on them.

But Issy let him know, *it's more of a fluid motion.*

Taking a deep breath, he tried again, carefully swiping his hand over the keypad slowly but without faltering. The pad flashed green and he could hear the click of the lock. He pushed the door open and they descended into the belly of the beast.

CHAPTER 17

Down and down they went. Moss wondered how many floors of cadets and trainees they passed.

"Always thought that if I was going down the stairs," Issy said quietly, "that it would be because I was being promoted to a Zeta."

"You wanted to be one of those?" Ynna asked in shock.

Issy let out a theatrical laugh. "Where you think you would be right now if you hadn't caught your dad fucking that robot?"

"Touché," Ynna said. She always seemed to respect it when someone gave as good as they got.

"But really, I always wanted to be good at what I did and becoming a Zeta was the dream. It meant you had arrived."

"It's funny, that," Judy said. "All these companies set up these rail systems for their employees. They hop on, sit down, and ride out the rest of their lives always feeling like they're moving forward, when really it's just a circle."

Moss considered their words. They were right and he thought about how easily it could have been his life if not for that one detour that ended in a complete derailment. As they reached the bottom of the stairs, Moss turned and looked at his armored friends.

"You guys ready for this?"

Nods all around and he waved his hand over the keypad. The door dinged and he pushed his way in, gripping the weapon holstered at his hip. The door opened to a large circular space dimly lit with low green lights running around the floor and ceiling. A hologram at the center of the room displayed a BurbSec Zeta with dates underneath indicating that this particular soldier had lost his life. It faded out and another replaced them . . . and on and on.

Without saying a word, everybody branched off in different directions. Issy and Gibbs made their way towards the barracks; Ynna, protecting Patchwork, moved toward the control room while Moss and Judy headed to the armory.

"This can be huge, you know?" Judy said as they pushed the door to the hallway open. It was as dimly lit as the main room had been, and several doors stood close together along both walls. The space was unadorned, setting a somber and serious mood, the kind of mood you wanted to set for these kinds of soldiers.

"Huge if we survive," Moss observed.

"Yeah. There really are so few of us left now."

"Seriously," Moss said and stopped, turning to face Judy. "Hey, Jude —"

But they cut them off.

"I'm okay," they said, and Moss wished he could see their expression under the helmet. "Really, I am. It's just seeing that store that got me. I told you I'm doing better, but every now and again it's gonna come back at me. Your brain all right?"

"You mean the program or me?"

Judy chuckled. "Either or, I suppose."

"I'm okay, too," Moss said. "It's just this life, what we do and how we live, it takes a toll. You know that better than anyone and it's finally starting to catch up with me too."

"I get it," Judy said, and Moss knew they meant it. "Maybe after D2E, you and Issy could take a quick break. Get outta here like Gibbs and Ynna just did. Some space might do you good."

Moss thought about it and really liked the idea. He knew there were a thousand reasons not to, but he didn't care about any of them. He had this one life and if they could take down the head of D2E and use their network to expose ThutoCo after crippling its army, he *would* deserve some time off. Of course, he would first have to do all of those things and still be alive at their completion.

He opened his mouth to respond but they heard voices coming from down the hallway and fell silent. Looking around, Moss found an unmarked door and waved his hand in front of the keypad. It dinged and opened, and they ducked inside what turned out to be a janitor's closet. The cleaning drudge sat on its charging pad beside a wire rack of cleaning supplies. Manually, Moss closed the door just enough so he could watch as the Zetas passed by.

"It's just one thing after another," one of them groused.

"I know," the other answered. "Ever since that meeting it feels like management is all over the place. But I think once we have the network, everyone is going to be in better shape."

"Here's hoping," said the first. "Man, did you catch Johnny Mukazi on *Skillz All-Stars* last night?"

"Yes!" and the voices became muffled as they rounded a corner.

"Shiiiiiit," Moss exhaled, turning to Judy in the cramped space.

They shook their head. "If they take the detritus network," Judy paused, clearly considering the horrors, "all of this will have been for nothing. They can just move in and take Carcer's place. They can see that Mix LeBeau is killed or removed from power…"

"Well," Moss said, "it's a good thing were here to destroy their base and cripple their ability to attack us."

Judy patted Moss on the back. "Let's do it then."

They pushed back out into the hallway and continued toward the armory. If they were caught at this point the jig would be up, so they pulled their weapons out and were ready for action. With the other teams moving simultaneously, anyone could set off an alarm and the situation would change for all of them.

At the control room, Patchwork informed them. *Starting the break now.*

That was good news, but it meant that the cameras were still online so when they heard footsteps, once again, they had to duck into the first available door. They watched a Zeta move past them quickly. But as Moss began to turn to share a moment of relief with Judy, they pressed their finger to the mouthpiece of their helmet and Moss saw why. They were in a room full of cots and Zetas lay sleeping all around them.

Judy began to move quietly towards the door but Moss shook his head. Judy cocked their helmet by way of question and Moss held up his Kingfisher, making a show of clicking it to stun. They nodded in understanding and pulled out their own weapon, pilfered from the ThutoCo van. Judy hooked a thumb to the left and Moss aimed his weapon to the right, before holding up his other gloved hand and raising three fingers. He dropped them in quick succession and the room began to flash with bluc lights as they fired. If things went sideways, this would make it a lot easier.

All of the soldiers in their sleepwear went from peaceful slumber to knocked out in an instant and the room smelled vaguely of cooked chicken. Moss watched Judy's head snap up to look to the corner of the room and he chuckled.

"BurbSec doesn't have cameras in the bedrooms or bathrooms," he said. "Issy once went on a tirade about a bunkmate who was always masturbating, but they couldn't bring him up on charges because it wasn't on camera. Meanwhile, in our hexes, they were more than happy to film our every —"

"All due respect, I got the relevant information," Judy said, and Moss nodded. He reached down and plucked up one of the Zeta's gloves, tossing it to Judy before grabbing another for himself. They both replaced the ones they had on.

"This'll help," Moss said.

"It's funny," Judy said contemplatively as they gazed down at the Zetas. "When we are sleeping, no amount of training makes any difference."

"Could be argued that we just took down a bunch of unarmed people," Moss said as he moved towards the door.

"These fuckers are agents of a structure of systematic oppression perpetrated on the citizens of B.A. City, but yeah, let's make sure they're given a fair fight."

Moss chuckled and held up his hands defensively as he pushed the door open with his hip. Back in the hallway, they rounded another corner and saw a lighted sign for the armory. Unlike the sleeping quarters, Moss knew there would be cameras in this room. *Armory cameras,* he requested of Patchwork.

Looped, five inside but unawares, he responded and he and Judy pressed themselves against the wall on either side of the door. Once again, Moss counted down with his fingers and waved his new glove over the keypad. He took a deep breath and shouldered his way through the door with Judy right beside him.

Unlike the rest of the space, the armory was well lit, and under different circumstances would have been a treasure trove. Freshly printed armor lined the walls and racks upon racks of guns, grenades, and tools filled the center of the space. They could have supplied an entire army with just the contents of this room — which was why it needed to be destroyed.

All the heads turned and Moss and Judy both took shots, but where the average BurbSec officer would have been taken unawares, the Zetas has had lightning quick reflexes. One was dropped but the other dodged and all of them were reaching for their weapons in an instant. Moss dove behind a crate that he hoped wasn't full of explosives, but as he rattled to the ground he remembered that he had some strapped to his chest.

Judy moved left behind the weapons rack and cleverly fired between the guns, blasting one of the Zetas who fell to the ground smoking and sizzling. That was when Moss remembered that when a Zeta's armor detected no life signs, it destroyed the evidence of its existence and that of its wearer's.

The wall behind Moss began to sizzle and crack as relentless onslaught of fired bolts cascaded all around. He would normally wait for his enemies to reload but the three remaining Zetas were clever – one was always firing while the others were reloading so there was a constant hail. Turning his head, he saw a rack of Turaco rifles. The Kingfisher subsidiary was notorious for making crappy weapons and Moss smiled under his helmet. He flipped the switch on his Kingfisher and shot out the legs of the rack, sending the rifles clattering to the ground and, as he had hoped, setting several of them off.

He and Judy had to duck as rifle fire peppered the room, but Moss heard one of the Zetas cry out in pain as he was hit with a bullet and his volley stopped. Moss popped out from behind a crate and took another shot before the other Zetas recovered and began firing back. Judy had the one that was on the ground. Seeing that he was outnumbered, the last remaining Zeta dove and rolled before his armor shimmered into invisibility.

Moss knew the advanced Dermidos technology wouldn't stay exclusive forever, but he certainly hadn't expected it to make its way onto ThutoCo armor so soon.

"There are two of us and just one of you," Judy called out by way of threat, but Moss knew they were just trying to coax the Zeta into talking. Unfortunately, the special operative didn't fall for it, nor did he make a sound when he moved. Moss crouched behind a box but knew he couldn't stay there for long. He considered having Patch use a thermal display and call out the Zeta's position but thought better of it. If used a live feed during a firefight, ThutoCo HQ would get wise immediately and their whole plan would be for nothing.

He popped back out and took a couple of shots but didn't hit anything. A sense of terror began growing in him as he realized that the Zeta could just walk right over and shoot Moss in the face without him being any the wiser. He had to do something.

He reached for one of the Turacos and dragged it into his position. Quickly, he shifted onto his back and began firing into the ceiling, sending dust, bits of debris and chunks of ceiling crashing to the ground. The gray dust began to settle on everything in the room but as Moss moved to take his shot, he felt a blow against his helmet. He let out a quick exhalation as he crashed down onto his side from his knees.

A blurry shape moved around the crate, raising its weapon. The dust covering the digital armor made the Zeta look like a ghost hunting Moss to his grave. But his plan had worked.

Judy could now see the soldier and shot him through the neck. He quickly raised his hands but it was far too late. A mist of blood rained down on Moss as the Zeta fell to his knees before slumping backwards.

As all the bodies and armor began to vaporize from the inside, a smell so putrid filled the space Moss and Judy could smell it through the filters in their helmets. Moss quickly unstrapped the chest plate and pulled the explosives from his body. Looking at Judy, he said, "You get to wear bombs to a gunfight next time."

Judy pulled their helmet off and gasped for air as though the thing were restricting their ability to breathe. "No, thank you," they said with a little smirk.

"Ah, I see. My value as the figurehead of a revolution doesn't extend to keeping me from having to wear this shit?" he snorted as he began to cut away the duct tape and pull off the explosives.

"It does not," Judy said flatly.

"Also," Moss said as he pulled his own helmet off, "you know what I'm getting sick of?"

"I have a guess," Judy said, coming to help Moss with the explosives.

"Hit me with it," Moss said as Judy began to set the charges.

"You're sick of getting shot at all the time."

Moss's mouth fell open. "That's exactly right. How did you know?"

"Because we're literally getting shot at all the time," Judy said as though it was the most obvious thing in the world. "To say nothing of the fact that your girlfriend was hospitalized because of it recently."

"I guess I just hate being that predictable," Moss said.

Judy looked at him incredulously. "Moss, my friend, you are a great many things, Unpredictable is not among them."

Moss made a show of covering his heart as though he'd been struck by an arrow and took great offense. "I'm sure you didn't see that weapon rack coming."

Judy looked up from where they were setting the explosives by a rack full of grenades, "You are right about that."

Moss smiled triumphantly and Judy rolled their eyes. "Charges are all set."

"Let's blow this banana stand," Moss said with a grin.

Judy rolled their eyes again, this time even more dramatically. "That's not even the expression."

CHAPTER 18

They hurried down the hallway away from the charges toward the main room, where they saw the others entering as well. Thumbs shot up all around and they began to make their way towards the exit.

"I think it's time," Moss told Patchwork, who nodded.

They put their helmets back on and Moss heard in his mind, *okay, Detritus Twenty-One, light 'em up.*

They heard nothing in response for a long time, but as they began to make their way up the stairs toward the main part of the facility, they heard the wailing of sirens. They readied themselves once again and Moss pushed the door open.

BurbSec officers and cadets were rushing toward the new action outside. Some were in half-assembled armor; others carried their weapons incorrectly and still others were in nothing but their sleeping linens.

Seeing all this, Ynna turned to Issy and said, "Well, shit, you would been promoted in no time."

"I know, right?"

They all fell in with all the BurbSec soldiers, running alongside them and making their way to where Tak and his crew were assaulting the facility, firing shots from positions near blown-out chunks of the wall separating the warehouse from the street. The BurbSec cadets had raised a small wall from the ground which had been installed for this very reason – to provide cover during an invasion.

More soldiers rushed past them as they fell into position and Moss and his team just looked at their backs. Moss turned to look at his friends and said, "I almost feel bad."

"'Almost' being the operative word," Ynna said, and Moss could hear the smirk.

Moss nodded as everybody raised their weapons toward the hapless line of BurbSec soldiers. He pressed the button on the detonator, and after a moment the earth shook. At the same time, Judy, Patchwork, Gibbs, Ynna and Issy opened fire. In accordance with Issy's needs, both they and Detritus Twenty-One were using nonlethal ammunition, knocking them unconscious in rapid succession. Surrounded on both sides, BurbSec didn't stand a chance and were all dropped in short order. After a moment, Moss was waving a friendly greeting to Tak from the other side of a column of knocked-out BurbSec soldiers.

"To another nail in the coffin of the megas," Moss said, raising a glass. In the new safehouse, the two crews all cheered and cheersed. "Today was a huge victory for all of us. It cost us a lot, including our home, but it was worth it to show ThutoCo that they are no longer welcome here. With our mayor in place, Carcer gone, ThutoCo on its heels and D2E soon to be crippled as well, our time is at hand. The next part of the road will be arduous, but we will see it done and usher in a new dawn for B.A. City and all the inhabitants of earth."

Another round of cheers went up and Moss smiled. After so much self-doubt and so much worry about the future, it was nice to experiencee a victory. They all needed it and Moss knew he needed it most.

Everyone began drinking and partying and Moss smiled to see it. Tak had also been right. The new place was much better than the old. Hidden away in a wide-open space that had once been some subterranean rapid transit system, the safe house was lovely. Everyone had their own tent, there were working bathrooms and Tak had even rigged it with entertainment and heating systems.

"Between this new place and sticking it to our old employer, it's hard not to feel good," Issy said as she walked over. She laced her fingers into Moss's and stood up on her tiptoes to kiss him on the cheek. He smiled and kissed her on the top of her head.

"Pretty sure that means that one of us is about to die," he half-joked.

She slapped him on the chest and said, "Don't even joke about that."

"Think it's just a coping mechanism."

"Or defense mechanism."

Moss chuckled. "Maybe both."

Issy led Moss toward the tent they shared, pulling open the flap and him down on the couch. A holoprojected screen was showing old movies in the corner and an air purifier kept the space from getting too stale or hot. There was a small bed, plastic shelving unit for clothes, a little desk with a chair and the small couch on which they sat. They had lost everything they had owned, but it hadn't been much so neither were that disappointed. Issy had joked that it would just give her an opportunity to go shopping.

"I've been thinking a lot about the future," Moss said, gazing into Issy's eyes.

A crooked little smile crossed her lips. "Yeah?"

"Yeah," Moss said and a clever little smile crossed his lips. "I spoke to my friend at The Conservation while you were recovering."

He watched the disappointment wash over her as he continued. "He believes it will be impossible to ever return the planet to the way it once was, especially with the vast number of people on the earth, but we will be able to help begin the healing process. He also told me there's a lot more wilderness left then I realized. While there's a lot to be pessimistic about, we really might be able to do something remarkable when all this is done."

"That's great," Issy said, forcing a smile. "Really great."

She looked away a moment and, though they were holding hands, she was distant and disconnected. He gave her hand a squeeze and she turned back to him.

"That wasn't the only future, though."

She smiled and he slid off the couch and down onto one knee. "Issy," he said quietly, trying to find the right words. "I've wanted to marry you since I understood that marriage was a thing. I still wanted to marry you when I realized it was kind of a farce and I desperately wanted to marry you when I realized you loved me too.

"You are the eye of the tornado – you keep me sane when the world is being ripped up around me. You are my strength, my light and … my everything."

Issy slid onto the ground so they were face to face, tears streaming down her cheeks and a bright smile on her lips. Never one to let him finish his speech, she said, "Moss, I've loved you since before I knew what romantic love was. When we were kids, I wanted you to crawl into my bed to keep me safe, and when we were older, for other reasons. You've always made my world more interesting, made my life complicated, hard, and worth living. Without you, I would have lived and died without ever having experienced anything, and even though I may have experienced *too much* because of you, I wouldn't have had it any other way.

"And, anyway, hopefully after this you won't have to have sex with robot versions of me," she said, sniffling before a massive grin crossed her face and she giggled at her own joke.

Moss felt his face flush and contort before he said, "Ugh, you bring that up during my proposal?"

"I don't see no ring," Issy said, looking around flamboyantly.

He reached into his pocket, and as he did, he closed his eyes briefly and braced his brain. He felt it just as he knew he would – the slamming from inside his mind. He was starting to sense when it would happen. He didn't know if that was a good or a bad thing, but at least he wasn't getting knocked on his ass as he was trying to ask Issy to marry him.

Swallowing hard, he pulled the ring from his pocket. As Issy's eyes lit up he felt a knot form in his stomach.

"It was my mother's. It was in a bag given to me when the company told me that my parents had died. I never thought I would do anything with it and certainly never expected I would be lucky enough to give it to you … but … oh, fuck it, Issy, will you marry me?"

"Yes!" she nearly shouted and plucked the ring from his hand, sliding it onto her finger.

Through tears, she looked down at the ring on her hand, beaming. Moss's heart felt full and he pulled her into an embrace, kissing her on the cheek. She pulled back and returned the kiss.

He knew this was what he needed. He needed some optimism, something in his life to look forward to, to make everything they had done feel worthwhile. His entire life couldn't be just about finishing some fight his parents had started. It needed to be about him and the people he loved as well. He didn't know what a wedding would look like nor when it could be, but he was happy that he could share a moment with Issy. This moment.

"And," he croaked through his own tears of joy, "I was thinking that after we deal with D2E, you and I can take some time off. Even if it's just a week. I want to spend some time together, just the two of us."

"That sounds amazing. I'll invite my dad, too," Issy joked, and it took Moss a moment to realize that she was only kidding but then he laughed.

"Oh, good, just what I've always wanted."

They spent several moments just looking at each another. They were both happy and, in a weird way, felt safe. They were winning in every sense of the word, and for the first time ever, Moss felt they might be able to achieve what they had set out to do.

"So, like, do we have to have sex now, or something? Or can I go tell everyone?" Issy asked hopefully.

"Oh," Moss said in surprise. "Was sex on the table?"

Issy sprang up and said over her shoulder as she made her way to the door, "Not anymore."

Moss followed her out, watching as she walked toward the throng with her hand outstretched in the telltale pose of an engagement announcement. Everyone turned and began cheering, and Ynna rushed over to wrap her in her arms right before Gibbs did the same. Moss heard her talking and happily bragging, explaining who she was to the members of the other crew, as Gibbs separated himself and slinked over to Moss.

"Copycat," he said as he moved in next to Moss and bumped shoulders.

"Right. It was you and not the thousands of years of tradition or my undying love that inspired me."

"Whatever. We both know the truth." Gibbs grinned.

Moss laughed and his friend wrapped him in an embrace. "I'm so happy for you, man."

"Thanks," Moss said. "We are quite grown up now."

"Happened quickly," Gibbs observed.

"I don't know, man, the last few years have felt like several people's lifetimes."

"You are not wrong about that."

"Anything I need to know about married life?"

Gibbs smirked. "It's all psychological."

"How's that?"

"Nothing is different in any way, but in some monumental way in your mind, things are different. It's like a feeling … I don't know how to describe it."

Moss looked at his friend and felt that he somehow understood.

"Plus," Gibbs said, "I've only been married for like a minute."

"That's a fair point," Moss chuckled and as he looked at Ynna, he saw a shaky little white dog move to nuzzle at her legs.

"Perro survived?" Moss gasped.

Gibbs rolled his eyes. "That thing'll outlive us all. And let's be real, if those guys had killed the dog, Ynna would be coating the earth in their blood."

The two men covered their words with smiles as Ynna tuned to look at them and came skipping over.

"And here she comes now," Moss said as he waved his hand as if to present her to Gibbs. Seeing what he was doing, she even made more of a show of walking over, spreading her arms wide as though she was a famous dignitary.

When she got close, she punched Moss in the shoulder and smiled. It hurt, but he was happy that at least it was with her human hand. "Congratulations," Ynna said with a genuine smile. "Ownership of Isabella officially can transfer from her father to you."

Moss groaned but didn't say anything in response.

"See, dumbass," she said to Gibbs, "if you don't take the bait, I got no other play." She turned back to Moss. "Seriously, congratulations."

"Thanks."

"And to think," she said, looking him right in the eyes, "you wanted to fuck me so bad when we first met."

"What? No! Wait, what? It wasn't like that," Moss stammered, and amusement grew on Ynna's face.

She laughed in his face. "For one, I know the look of a guy who wants to break into my database." Moss felt himself flush, but mercifully she turned to Gibbs and said, "As always, he's as easy to fuck with as you are."

Moss and Gibbs both looked at her with visible annoyance and she crinkled her face. "You two are no fun."

"Then I have bad news for you," Gibbs said.

"The bad news is you married one … har, har, har," she mocked but a small smile crossed her face. Gibbs tapped his finger to his nose and winked. And Ynna grumbled, "Why do I like you?",

"We're all still wondering that," Moss said.

Gibbs wrapped his arm around Ynna and made a pouty face. "How did this become about me?"

"I thought you always wanted it to be about you," Moss said.

"Ooh, burn, Gibbs," Ynna laughed and squeezed his cheeks. Turning to Moss, she said, "I'm really happy for you guys."

"Thanks," Moss said and clinked his glass against hers.

"Thought about when and where to have the wedding?" She asked as though she was being casual, but Moss could tell she would report back to Issy the next second if she got some intel.

Moss shrugged. "Got any suggestions?"

"Well, if we manage to finish this, you can actually have it out the open," Ynna suggested and Moss wanted to laugh before realizing that it was probably true.

"Wow," he murmured, taking in the gravity of it.

"Yeah," Ynna said quietly. She turned and caught sight of Judy having a drink in the corner after having extricated themselves from the group. "Should probably go talk to them."

"I will. Thanks, guys."

"Ball busting aside," Ynna said, "we are really happy and love you guys."

"Right back at you," he said and made his way across the space. He glanced over at a map mounted on the tile wall that had colored lines representing different routes the old subterranean rail system used to take.

He continued to gaze at the map as he sidled up to Judy and said, "Crazy to think what this old system looked like back in the day."

"Don't need kid gloves, Moss," they said without looking at him. "I can say congratulations and you know I mean it, no matter how hard it might be for me."

"I know," Moss said, and he really did. He knew that they loved both himself and Issy and was truly happy for them, but also knew how hard it was. "I just wish … I just wish you could have some closure so that all this joy didn't have the side product of hurting you."

"Me too," Judy said through gritted teeth. Then they turned red eyes on Moss. "But I'll never have closure knowing that he's just rotting in some mass grave. Given his beliefs, it's just not right."

"I know," Moss said quietly.

A single tear rolled down their cheek before they wiped it away quickly on a sleeve. "I really am so happy for you. You deserve this. You both do."

Moss smiled and they chatted a while longer until a voice in his head piped in, *Moss*, Seti said, *our man inside D2E has set the meeting*.

PART 3

CHAPTER 19

Moss felt odd in his new suit. The Tailor had made it to fit him perfectly, but he felt more comfortable in his ratty old clothes. He liked the way it looked and liked the way Issy reacted to him even more, so he tolerated it. Plus, it was allowing him to walk into a building he would never have otherwise been able to enter: The Silver Screen, D2E's corporate office.

It was in the southern part of the city where most of the city's media content was produced. The building was wider than it was tall and designed so that the office windows were all digital displays. The entire front and back of the building constantly streamied trailers for their movies.

Massive speakers wound around all the surrounding buildings, so there was no place you would walk within blocks of The Silver Screen without being fed some of the media content. An action movie crashed and exploded overhead, and Moss couldn't help but watch as he walked down the street toward the building. Pretty people schmoozed business folks in their suits as others sat in cafés, trying to be seen writing their scripts on their tablets. Expensive cars rolled up and down the street and Moss realized that every single person here was trying to get attention.

Everyone, except him. Despite being among the most famous people on earth, in a suit and with sunglasses he blended right into the background. He approached the studio steps and began making his way up past the statues of famous and influential filmmakers. As he ascended, Moss passed a man screaming into his palm screen and he wondered why he wouldn't just use some form of neural communication before he realized that he was trying to make a show of himself.

Moss shook his head before he heard, "Mr. Scott, welcome to D2E!"

Looking up, Moss saw a young, stylish man waving to him from the top of the stairs. Moss lifted a hand in acknowledgment and moved towards him. "Hi, I'm Bela, personal assistant to Mr. Von 'Tude."

"Good to meet you," Moss said, extending a hand.

Bela had dark microdyed hair that shimmered and moved like waves in the light. He wore mirror shades and a large, gaudy watch set with diamonds in the face. He appeared to Moss that he had only just started shaving, and he smelled so strongly of cologne that Moss felt a tickle in his nose.

"Have you had any meetings here with us before?" he asked, and though he was talking to Moss, he was also obviously working. His fingers tapped away at his palmscreen and his eyes were vacant.

"I have not. Never thought I had a story worth telling."

"Oh, that's so cute. They love self-deprecation up there," Bela said with a little hand motion before turning to walk up the stairs toward the building. Though it was day, the light from the screens still shone on them and the images danced in the reflected fields over the young man's eyes.

As they passed through the doors, striding right past the hired security, Moss couldn't help but feel odd. Every time he found himself in this position, walking around in some corporate headquarters, he was always in the middle of a firefight or using some disguise; but not this time. Now, he was just walking in as a person. It was refreshing. Still, he didn't expect to have too many more experiences like this.

The interior of the building was designed to look like an old-style movie theater with digital red displays above the doors, large leather seats with cupholders in the waiting area, a popcorn machine and backlit posters throughout the headquarters. Moss had to admit it was actually pretty fun and knew Gibbs would have loved it. One entire wall was occupied by gold statues that Moss assumed meant something important to the studio.

Bela seemed to catch his look as he glanced up just for a moment from his work. "We have more awards than any of the other major studios."

"It's impressive," Moss said as they made their way toward the bank of elevators.

"It really is," Bela said in a tone that made Moss feel as if he was being corrected. "Don't believe the people who tell you it was all because we absorbed that *other* company. We have had some really successful releases on our own."

"Okay," Moss said, not entirely sure what this kid was getting at.

Bela turned after pressing the elevator button and looked right at Moss. "Look, we may be known for our blockbusters, but we also make some powerful smaller works that ask questions about the nature of humanity. It's deep, cutting-edge stuff, all right?"

Moss smiled. "Sounds great."

"It *is* great," Bela said before disappearing back into his work. Moss couldn't help but find it amusing how seriously this young man took his job. It was meaningless. All of this was meaningless. The studio churned out unimportant entertainment to make slaves of the masses, and yet this kid thought he was creating high art. He was either delusional or a fantastic liar — or perhaps such a fantastic liar that he was perfectly self-delusional.

They got into the elevator and rode for a long time, and Moss's stomach turned for a moment. But soon the door dinged, and Moss was following the young man down a long hallway full of doors leading to offices. What was strange was how familiar it all was. Working in the burbs felt like another life but being here brought it all back. You might as well just be walking to Mr. Greene's office to tell them about getting MOSS II stuck in a ditch. Because, when all was said and done, he had been that version of himself for a lot longer than this version.

At the end of the hall was a door with Rude Von 'Tude spray-painted on its front. Beside it was a whiskey vending machine, and Moss turned to Bela with an inquisitive look. The young man looked up and caught his eye.

"Rude wants everybody feeling good before they enter his office."

"I have to take a shot to go in?"

The young man just gave him a blank look. He walked over and pressed the dispense button, waiting a moment as a small paper cup plopped down before being filled with brown liquid. Moss tossed it back in one gulp and turned back to Bela, who smiled briefly and pressed a button on his palm screen. Moss had never seen someone use a screen quite as actively as this young man. Most people just seemed to veg out, watching the screen digitally meshed into their hand, but Bela was tapping away at it always, his fingers looking like dancing spider legs.

The door opened and Moss entered the room. Rude smiled up from where he was sitting behind his desk. The entire place was a shrine to himself. All four walls showed different episodes of his show and he was reviewing an episode that was undoubtedly going to air today on a screen projector from his desk. He sat in a throne-like chair complete with gold trim and red velvet. There were barstools set across the desk facing him and Moss took one of those.

"Hey, man," Rude said, "like the touch with the booze?"

"I don't tend to turn down a drink, but I also don't tend to start my day at nine with some whiskey."

"I know, that's what's so amazing about it." Rude grinned like a child. "Seeing all these uptight suits only being able to open my door after having to drink booze first thing in the morning, that some funny shit right there."

"You certainly do have a unique way of thinking," Moss offered.

"That I do," Rude said as he stood up, giving Moss a good look at his shirt. It bore the words 'Show Your,' followed by a picture of a cat. Rude smiled as he saw Moss staring. "That's my cat."

"That's nice," Moss said, wishing the man would get to the business at hand.

"And what's wild," Rude began excitedly, "is that about once a day somebody does."

Moss nearly asked what before realizing and just said, "Okay."

Sensing Moss's disinterest, Rude turned the page. "You ready for this?"

"What is this? Moss asked.

"I got you a meeting with Derek Sterling," Rude told him and Moss knew the pressure was really on now. Being here was one thing, but he had to steel himself for a meeting with one of the heads of the world's largest companies and a member of the AIC. "He thinks this is so you can pitch him a new show concept but it's actually so that —"

Moss held up a hand and didn't say a word but sent the man a look that told him to keep his mouth shut. Rude nodded.

"So, you have your meeting and it will just be the two of you. Security will be in the room. Once you guys finish your conversation, you can bring his access card and we can take over the signal …"

"Understood," Moss said, pleased that D2E and Derek Sterling would pay for what they had been doing. ThutoCo had just paid for their actions and now another one of the companies would too.

Rude came around and leaned on his desk, affecting the serious look that he had taken before he and Moss had spoken normally. "Do you know you're going to say?"

This was something that Moss had been thinking about a lot. He had waffled, questioned himself and considered only telling part of the truth. But he knew he had to tell everyone the full truth from now on.

"Yes. We are going to tell the world everything that ThutoCo has done. We are going to tell them that they poisoned the planet and forced everybody to live inside the walls of the city. We are going to tell them that they took over all the land and told people it was poisoned, but they had cured their self-made plague long ago. We are going to tell them that they planned to release the disease again if they had to, and even did a trial run on their own people. We are going to present them with proof. Along with the broadcast, we will be filling the internet with clips and stories from the scubas. There are

ThutoCo expats who will talk about what has happened. Irrefutable proof from every angle, all at once. They might try to say it's false, but it'll be too much and from too many places."

Rude didn't break eye contact the entire time. He just listened intently. "Oh yeah, when everyone got ill a few years back. An entire work force all laid out, the whole place stinking of sick ... wow ... when you put it all together, it's some really dark shit."

"It really is," Moss said. "That's why it's nice to say it all together like that, to remind myself why we're doing this."

"What you think's gonna happen?"

"I'm hoping the people come to our aid, the way they did against Carcer. I'm hoping that exposing ThutoCo and the whole AIC makes people mad enough to join us once again and get these companies out of here once and for all. I'm hoping ..." and he paused, realizing what he really wanted. "I'm hoping the natural life gets its planet back – in every sense."

"Lofty ambition," Rude said with quiet admiration. "If anyone can do it though, I expect it's you."

"Thank you," Moss said, standing, and Rude extended a hand. Moss took it and they shook. "You taking me?"

"Yeah, let's go kill this cocksucker."

CHAPTER 20

"Twice in one week," Moss noted as he and his grandmother entered the sewers.

Moss and Rude didn't speak as they rode up to the top floor. Every now and again, Moss would glance at the older man, seeing the wrinkles that had crept in and the grays that hadn't been dyed away, and Moss wondered what it would be like to be this aging relic of some bygone time. Though Patchwork still seemed enamored of him, Rude's time in the sun was obviously behind him; but he still had to be this thing, play this character for the rest of his life.

Moss wondered if that would be him too, if he would have to be this thing even when it was all over. He wanted a simple life, a free life. He hoped he could. Having proposed to Issy, he needed to believe that he would be able to spend part of his life with her. Not just a week between deadly missions, but his life.

That thought carried him forward as the elevator doors opened and he strode out into a glass tunnel. Rude needed an access card to ride to this floor and Moss realized the corridor led directly to Derek's office.

The glass hall was fused so perfectly it felt like you were walking on air over the city. Looking left and right stopped Moss's heart; he wanted to drop to the ground and crawl to the office. He had never quite acclimated to heights like this. Even flying over the city with drone packs and climbing the tallest tower had not prepared him for the sense of being suspended over the city.

He didn't let it show and just walked forward. At about the halfway point, he felt a slam on his back and nearly dropped to his knees. His arms darted straight out and he braced himself against the glass, his whole body shaking.

"Scary, huh?" Rude laughed as he continued to pat Moss on the back.

The moment gave Moss pause. He wondered if Rude was fundamentally a bad person who had made a career out of being an asshole. At least the man was doing one good thing with his life, Moss considered as he trudged forward.

After what felt like an eternity, he was on the other side. A large waiting room with several screens showed many of D2E's networks simultaneously around a large desk with a personal assistant behind it. Several beefy ex-Carcer officers stood by the door to the office . Just like the tunnel, all the walls were glass.

Moss wandered to one corner, where he saw some birds had made a nest on a little outcropping. As he got closer, he saw they were gray birds of preys, pigeon hawks. These birds had been created and bred to deal with the pigeon population. He watched the big female preen a bit, pulling a feather into her beak to clean it. The animal was beautiful, powerful and, in that moment, so peaceful. But he could see the bits of dried blood on her talons that told him what she really was – a killer.

Moss pulled his collar, smoothed his suit jacket and walked over to Rude, who was indicating for him to step into the office. He extended a hand, and Moss took it.

"Good luck with the pitch," Rude said loudly so that the guards would buy the lie.

The two bruisers in their ill-fitting suits pulled the swinging double doors open and Moss stepped into a small anteroom. It was simple, furnished with two chairs, a watercooler and a small fern in the corner. The doors closed behind him and, to Moss's great pleasure, there were actual walls. He only had to wait a moment before the second set of doors opened.

He turned and his mouth fell open. He stepped right to the edge of the anteroom and looked around. The area spreading before him was massive, but it wasn't really a room. Much like the feudal Japanese apartment, the office was another trick of the mind. White sand stretched in three directions as waves lapped up on the shore to one side. Moss knew the digital walls made it seem that the beach stretched forever, but he couldn't tell where the room actually ended. Looking up, he couldn't tell if the area was topped by a glass or digital ceiling.

A man in his forties with shaggy blonde hair stepped out from a little cabana set in the middle of the beach. Instinctively, Moss kicked off his shoes before stepping into the sand. He had never really spent much time at a beach and hadn't smelled the ocean except from afar. The sand was soft beneath his feet, but the way it shifted was strange and took some getting used to as he walked toward Derek.

The head of D2E was dressed in baggy cargo shorts and an untucked button-up shirt. As he neared Moss, two chairs rose out of the sand between them. It was hot in the room and Moss began to sweat. Derek extended a hand.

"Mr. Scott, nice to meet you. Derek Sterling."

"A pleasure," Moss said, looking into the man's crystalline blue eyes. "This office is ... something ..."

Derek sighed, looking around. "Yeah, it's a bit much. I told the designer I wanted beach vibes and this is what I got," he said with a laugh. "Hard to say doesn't have 'beach vibes' though."

Moss couldn't help but laugh. "Got that right."

"It is certainly better than just four walls, but still a bit much." Derek signaled to the chairs and whispered conspiratorially, "Truth is, I have a regular office under this one, through the cabana. But this one always impresses investors."

Moss was surprised at how casual and open the man was. Even though he was one of the wealthiest men on the planet and a member of the AIC, he seemed completely down to earth. Most wondered if that was one of the ways he was able to fool people.

He sat on a beach chair across from Derek.

"Problem is," Derek continued, "sand and water get into everything. Cool as this is, the repair costs are immense."

"I can imagine," Moss said.

"Just getting all of this to the top of the building required more money in man-hours than I like to admit," Derek said with a rueful laugh. "Can I get you anything? Water, coffee? If you just came from Rude's office, I'm sure you need to replace that whiskey with something."

Moss chuckled. "No, I'm fine."

"Suit yourself," Derek said and when he smiled, Moss saw perfect white teeth. The man could have been a television star. He was tall and fit and had chiseled features. His perfectly imperfect five o'clock shadow was a look that Gibbs had tried to foster unsuccessfully for years. "So you're here to pitch me a new show. Well, you called this meeting, so let's hear the pitch."

"Actually," Moss said, "I'm here to ask you some questions." In a flash he pulled a specific seam at the cuff of his sleeve. The hidden garrote wire that had made it possible for him to pass through security slid out and Moss quickly had it around the man's neck.

Derek slipped one hand under the wire and began reaching for what Moss assumed to be a panic button under one of the chair's arms. Sand sprayed as Moss yanked Derek away from the chair before he could summon his security. The man thrashed and swung his hand at Moss. He made contact a few times but it didn't hurt much, so Moss kept pulling to subdue him.

But the man kept fighting. He pushed and pulled and yanked at Moss's clothing. The wire began to chew into his hand and blood sprayed everywhere as Moss tightened it. Soon, both were gasping for air and Moss's hands were beginning to hurt where he was gripping the wire. Derek slammed his head back in desperation and cracked one of Moss's ribs, staggering him just long enough for Derek to push himself away. Both toppled onto the sand.

Moss's hand came loose just long enough for Derek to jump to his feet. Oddly, he didn't make his way for the security button. Instead, he reached into his pocket and produced what looked like a black metal cylinder. He pressed the button and extended the metal bar, two knobs flitting out of the end. Derek smiled and moved towards Moss with an electrified cattle prod facing him.

"I grew up poor," Derek rasped. "I had to fight for everything I ever got. But they don't let me fight anymore."

"Happy to be of service," Moss said, wishing his suit had more hidden weapons. He had figured the wire would be enough and hadn't expected a fight, but he would deal with it. They circled each other for a while, both panting, and Derek dripping blood into the pristine sand.

Sweat poured down Moss's forehead and eventually he lunged, but Derek was too quick and jumped out of the way, managing to make contact with Moss's shoulder. He felt the electricity burn through it and winced, but quickly rolled out of the way and hopped to his feet.

Derek, excited at the moment of victory, lurched toward Moss swinging the prod. Moss ducked out of the way and tried to launch himself forward, but he was unprepared for the sand shifting under his feet and he fell flat to the ground.

Derek laughed. "What are you, some fucking bub?" he said pointing the prod at Moss's back. He rolled out of the way just in time, hearing the electricity sizzle into the sand.

Moss kicked the weapon out of Derek's hand. Backing up, Derek lifted both of his hands in balled fists, ready for a brawl. He no longer appeared the casual business leader. He looked like that kid who had grown up on the hard streets and had to scrape for everything he got.

Moss got up and lifted his own hands, ready for a fight.

"What do you want from me?" Derek demanded. "Money?"

"If I wanted money, I wouldn't have tried to kill you."

"Fair point," Derek said as they circled each other. "What, then?"

"Why?" Moss asked and Derek looked at him in confusion.

"Why what?"

"Why do you do this? What's your endgame? More money, just sheer power?"

It was a question he had wanted answered for so long. These men and women who controlled the world from the shadows: what was it that they were after?

Derek almost let his guard down for a moment as he looked at Moss in utter confusion. "You want to know the truth? I do it for all the kids like me. I do it so there don't have to be kids like me anymore."

He sounded sincere but Moss laughed. "You are the reason there are kids like you," he said and spat.

Derek roared and charged him. Moss tried to dive out of the way, but rage was carrying the man and he speared Moss in the stomach, knocking him to the ground. The sunglasses flew from Moss's face and Derek stopped, staring. He blinked and continued to stare. Moss was so dumbstruck by the man's face that he didn't fight back.

"Moss?" Derek said in genuine astonishment. "I'm a huge fan."

CHAPTER 21

"What?" Moss said. The moment defused in an instant and Derek stood, offering a hand to help Moss up.

"What you're doing, it's so remarkable," Derek said as his gesture turned into a gracious handshake. Derek was beaming at him. "I'm — I'm so sorry I attacked you."

"It's okay. I did try to kill you first."

"I suppose that's true," Derek said, chuckling. "Was that for show?"

Moss shook his head. His brain hurt. He didn't quite understand what was happening, but he knew it wasn't what it had seemed a moment earlier. Panting, he said, "Well, you're the head of an evil mega-corporation and a member of the Amalgamated Interests Council."

"Yeah," Derek said, still looking confused, "And?"

"And so I tried to kill you," Moss said.

"I'm your man on the inside," Derek said. Moss felt a headache like a vice grip. "Sandra never told you?"

Moss felt his blood begin to boil once again. "No," he said through gritted teeth. "She didn't tell me a lot of things."

"This *is* best kept secret," Derek said, seemingly trying to cover for Sandra. "If anyone found out — anyone — I would be dead. We needed to keep the tightest lid on this."

Moss's head was spinning. Derek ripped off a piece of his sleeve.

"Sorry again," Moss said, though he was lost in thought.

Derek pinched the cloth against his own bloody palm and began wrapping.

"It's fine. I wasn't kidding about wanting to get back to my roots."

Moss nodded, then blurted, "Wait a second, if we had a person on the fucking AIC, how come we didn't know all this stuff about ThutoCo? Why are we always chasing our tails?"

"Look, I'm sure you imagine that we all sit around planning world domination..." and here he chuckled, "and we kinda do, but that doesn't mean we share all our intel with one another. We don't talk about our schemes or our plans unless they benefit the whole, you know?

"Sure, we are theoretically on the same team, but we are all pulling in our own directions, too. While you were at war with everyone, we were at war with one another too. Shit, every company has its own agents to dispatch against the other companies while smiling at each other. Hard as it might be to believe, that's the reality of it."

Moss cracked a smile. "Makes sense, actually. I often wondered how we were able to do so much with so little. If the companies have to fear each other as much as they do us, I guess it adds up that we were able to get away with so much."

"Precisely," Derek said. "Plus you had me to stir up shit. Arthur Smith hates me as much as he does you."

"No wonder I liked you as soon as we met," Moss said and laughed.

It was a very odd moment — standing on a beach at the top of a building with a man who a moment earlier had been a mortal enemy. Moss couldn't help but think how strange his life had become.

"So," Derek said as he finished wrapping his hand and started marching towards the cabana. "Why are you here to kill me?"

Before Moss could answer, the sound of shattering glass grabbed his attention. Both men looked up and Moss saw exactly what he expected: more men in custom armor created by Gav.

"It's a set up!" Moss screamed and both men began running toward the cabana. Sand kicked up as glass electronics fell all around them, soon followed by bullets. The beach became a war zone as the soldiers with dronepacks dropped from the sky.

Moss was moving slowly, the suit and sand slowing him down. Derek moved quickly and easily up the beach, diving over the bar. Moss felt the impact of a bullet on his flank just below his ribs, and he had never been more thankful for anyone than he was for The Tailor. The impact of the projectile hurt but didn't break through the nanomesh suit.

Moss followed Derek over the bar into a hatch and down a metal ladder, pulling the door closed behind them and quickly spinning the locking mechanism. "You have a way out of here?"

"It's more of a panic room," Derek explained as he reached the landing.

When Moss hit the bottom, he saw a solid cement room, reinforced with steel walls and containing a small cot, couch, desk and a bank of monitors. It felt like a deathtrap.

Looking at the monitors, Moss saw the waiting room through which he had entered and the blood-spattered bodies of the guards within. On another screen, he watched as the agents above tried to break through the door. It would take them some time, but Moss knew they could get through.

"You have any weapons down here?"

"Yes, but I don't know how to use them," Derek said.

He rushed over to one of the steel panels on the wall and tapped it in a specific pattern. The door opened, revealing a small weapons locker. Moss smiled. It was all he needed.

Watching the monitors, Moss worked as quickly as he could to get everything situated. He grabbed weapon after weapon, relieved that whoever had stocked the room had thought of defense. Climbing up and down the ladder, Moss prepared as the armored agents got closer to cracking the door. He placed an unfolding base on the ground and activated it, the thing unfurling into a semicircular metal strip with sliding latches. It was just big enough to duck under and Moss got himself into position with a weapon.

Turning to Derek, who was standing there helplessly, he asked, "You trust me?"

The man nodded and Moss pointed at the small weapons locker. Though it was clear that he was terrified to do so, Derek walked over, stepped up onto the little lip and locked himself into the metal coffin. Moss didn't know how long the oxygen would last in there, although he hoped there was some type of supply, and knew he had to act fast.

Clanking and churning noises told him the agents were getting close. He wanted to pull his suit jacket off due to the heat in this confined space, but he wasn't willing to give up the little protection it provided. He flipped open one of the small hatches in the unfolding protective wall and pushed the barrel of the machine gun through.

Then heard it. The crack and the shouting. They were in.

The first agent began to descend and the first trip mine that Moss had set flashed before shredding him with an energy pulse. Bits of melted armor and gooey body dripped onto Moss's shield. More shouting came from above and Moss heard a scream as one of the agents was clearly pushed down the tunnel.

To Moss's dismay, it was a good plan, as it set off all of the remaining traps along the descent. The body of the agent was blasted with shrapnel, scorched with a flame burst and then punctured with a blunderblast. The body crashed to the ground in front of Moss and he heard more shouting. Another agent began to descend but Moss didn't open fire. He waited, biding his time.

Once there were four in the long, tight tunnel, Moss took aim. Closing one eye, he slowly exhaled, making sure he was spot on target, and pulled the trigger. The well-made weapon had no recoil and the bullets whizzed up the tunnel. With all the jostling and moving, it was hard to hit his exact target. Most of the bullets clanged off the agent's armor or slammed harmlessly into the wall but one, the one he needed, found a small chink in the armor.

It wasn't a kill shot, but it was enough and the man at the top of the line screamed and let go. His full weight came crashing down on the agent below him, who tried to keep his footing but couldn't. The two fell on the third and then all three on the fourth. All of them came crashing through the mouth of the tunnel and Moss opened fire.

He didn't blast them but took specific shots as they fell. Once they were down, he darted out from behind the shield and took them out in quick succession as they writhed on the floor. He was so pleased with his plan that he had almost forgotten there were more above. He was reminded when they opened fire on him, forcing him to dart back beneath his shield.

He quickly looked at the monitors and saw that there were only a few left. This time, they didn't try climbing down the ladder. They seem to have learned that this was a dire mistake and so all three jumped down, one after the other, using their dronepacks to break their fall. As soon as they cleared the lip, they started firing at the shield and didn't let up. Moss was pinned. He stayed in his position, trying to think what to do. He could tell they were moving around the sides, closing in around him.

He stuck the weapon around the side and fired blindly but he heard the bullets clang off the agents' armor. He had to pull his hand back before it was shredded.

Then the whole room shook and there was light and heat and screaming. Moss pressed his eyes closed and covered his head, but the shield did its work. There was a brutal ringing in his ears, and he could hardly breathe or see through the smoke and debris. He started coughing but didn't hear any more from the attackers. Flipping on the flashlight of the machine gun, Moss slid out from behind the shield, weapon pointed in the direction of the agents.

"Holy shit," he heard, and as he stepped forward, blinking hard, Moss could just make out Derek. "I just killed a whole bunch of people …" He said it more matter-of-factly than Moss would have expected. He figured the man was in shock.

"Yeah," Moss said. "Thanks for that."

"No problem." They both started to wave the dust away from their faces. "Who are these guys? Friends of yours?"

"Actually," Moss said, "friends of yours."

"How's that?" Derek asked as Moss realized they were shouting and choking and needed to get out of there. He began climbing the ladder once more, stepping on the pile of shredded bodies to get out.

Back on the beach, it looked a lot different under the crackling light of the broken digital ceiling mixed with the gray light from the real sky showing through the new gap. They both looked like garbage, covered in dirt and feeling half dead. Derek grabbed a bottle of pre-made piña colada and took a swig before handing it to Moss, who was happy just to get the dirt out of his mouth.

"These are friends of Rude Von 'Tude," he said slowly and watched as Derek's eyes went wide.

"What?"

"This whole thing was a setup to get us both killed," Moss told him. He had figured it out when the agents dropped through the roof. "Rude obviously has a family member, I'm guessing a wife or child, who works in the burbs. It didn't occur to me at the time, but he knew one too many details about an event that happened there. Sure, it was somewhat common knowledge, but he spoke about it as though he knew someone who experienced it. Of course, I only see that now...

"I'm guessing once ThutoCo realized who this relative was, it held them hostage and forced Rude to do their bidding. He convinced our people he wanted to be an agent in D2E, somehow figured out you were working with us, and led me on an investigation designed to point the finger at D2E. ThutoCo hired agents to start killing those folks funneling money to us so we wouldn't think it was them and let us find the armorer so he could lead us to you. ThutoCo found a way to shut down our money flow, you *and* me all in one fell swoop."

"Smart. But they weren't successful."

"No, they were not."

"So what can I do for you?"

"Let's get this story out there," Moss said. "Once and for all, let's tell everyone the truth. We have a bunch of content lined up, but it needs to come from an official source. That's going to be the key. It's the only way the world will believe what it hears."

"You sure about that?" Derek asked. "Your grandmother always seemed to think I was of more value on the inside than blowing my cover and going public."

"It's time," Moss said. "We hit their army, we have the momentum, and we have nothing else to lose. It's time to show the world what ThutoCo really is. It's time to end this."

Derek smiled and wiped off his palm with the rag around his other hand. He began typing, but then his face contorted in anger. "I'm locked out."

"Shit!" Moss exclaimed.

"He's in the control room with, I assume, ThutoCo breakers."

Seti, jam any D2E feed! Moss ordered as they both started running.

Copy that, Seti answered and asked Moss if he needed anything else, but he didn't answer. They had to get to the control room now. Whatever message Rude was planning to put out there was going to be bad.

They made their way through the anteroom, through the waiting room painted with blood and down the invisible tunnel to the elevator. Derek pressed the button several times but they were stuck waiting as the doors slowly closed and the elevator began to drop. Quiet music played, providing an odd moment of serenity.

"Stay behind me," Moss commanded as the door opened and he made his way out. There were bullet holes in the wall and nobody in the room, so Moss knew they were on the right track.

"Up that hall and to the right," Derek told him from behind.

Moss moved forward, his weapon pointing straight ahead. One of the agents emerged from a bathroom and Moss took a couple of shots, dropping her quickly. He knew they had the element of surprise. The agents would start to get curious soon when their friends didn't answer, but hopefully Moss could get to them first.

He felt a tap on his shoulder and Moss spun to pop off a few more shots at one of the agents coming around a corner. The silencer was doing a good job keeping the shots from reverberating through the building, but it didn't completely silence them and he knew that he would have to stop shooting as he approached the control room.

Soon it was within sight. Moss and Derek jogged forward.

As Moss elbowed the door open, all the agents turned as one to see him. He began firing and watched as the first two were blasted back. The third agent managed to get a few shots off from behind a consul full of screens and audio equipment and Moss had to brace himself as the impact knocked him back.

He felt as if he might have been injured but he didn't have time to check and he returned fire rapidly. He turned the muzzle on Rude who threw up his hands, looking terrified.

"I never wanted to do any of this," he yelled, already crying. "They made me. They made me!"

"You were right," Derek said. "Couldn't have scripted it better myself."

"What do they have on you?"

"My parents are bubs," Rude said quietly, keeping his shaking hands raised. "Once they realized that, they took them and made me do their bidding. First they interrogated me, then they made me go through with this."

"It's time you come clean," Derek said coldly.

"No!" Rude cried. "They'll kill them."

"They won't be able to once we go public with everything," Moss said. "Plus, you'll be the least of their problems."

Rude nodded slowly. He was spineless and Moss knew it. It was how ThutoCo had taken advantage of him and now Moss would too.

"How did you know who our people were?" Moss had to know.

"I gave you guys Rigg. He was a plant. He let us know who was using the scrubbed chips. ThutoCo would only take out some of the people helping you so that you guys didn't get wise and added the anarchist stuff just to keep you guessing."

"Fuck," Moss said. "Then they ravaged Rigg just to lead us to Gav so he could point at D2E?"

Again, the aging icon nodded. "You see how flippant they are with lives? That could be me. It could be my mommy …"

"We won't let that happen," Moss said. He gestured with his rifle toward the recording studio on the other side of the wall and said, "It's time. Rude Von 'Tude, you are about to become one of the most famous people on earth."

"Actually, I already was," Rude seemed unable to keep from saying.

"As a matter of fact, your ratings in even the eighteen to thirty-four demo have been trending down for the last several quarters —" Derek began but Moss cut him off.

"Unimportant," he snarled. "Now go. Go tell the world everything that ThutoCo has done."

Moss told him everything he needed to know and contacted Seti to ready the footage and proof to simultaneously disseminate online. As Rude made his way in front of the cameras, Moss's heart began to race.

This was it.

They were so close.

Moss was finally going to be able to do what he had wanted to since he had first learned what ThutoCo really was and how they were using his father's technology. It was all coming together. They would expose this company and all the others, and the world would join them in their fight.

Derek stepped over to the console array and began clacking away. He started counting down and Rude nodded. Moss felt his eyes begin to well as the green light went on and Rude began to speak.

A smile crossed his face.

It was happening. Rude was saying everything, telling the world everything.

As a tear rolled down his cheek, he turned to Derek, who was also smiling.

"Hey," Moss said. "Are you the mysterious benefactor of The Conservation?"

Derek smiled broadly. "I had only ever seen a pigeon and a raccoon until I was twenty. Like I said, I don't want any kids to have to grow up like me."

"Me neither," Moss said. "And after this, none will have to."

As Rude finished his speech and Derek showed Moss how many people were watching and sharing the story, Moss felt his heart soar. He thought about walking the streets of the city, seeing people watching their screens rather than where they were going, kids staring at their palms instead of playing.

He always hated to see it but now all those people were collectively his greatest weapon. He was harnessing their screen addiction to expose the company.

He had done it. He had outed ThutoCo and the AIC for what they were.

He had proposed to Issy and she had said yes.

His life was finally trending in the right direction.

He had done it for himself and for his family, and he wondered what they would say now.

Then he felt it.

He was slammed forward and his body crashed to the ground.

He blinked, trying to regain himself, but he felt the slam again. Blood sprayed from his mouth and this time when he blinked, the edges of his vision began to blur.

The room around him faded and soon he saw white.

He turned in his mind and there it was.

He had fought it for so long, kept it at bay for so long, but he was back in his digital hex.

In some ways, he was relieved. It had been so long, and he wondered if he would see his father.

As his head turned, he saw his dad briefly, but the man's face was red and contorted with rage.

His father grabbed him by the collar and slapped him across the face.

"How could you?" his father screamed, and the guilt and shame rose up in Moss.

His father hit him again. "How could you?" he repeated and punched Moss in the eye. It was in a program and Moss knew it, but it felt real and the feelings were real. His father hated him in this moment, and in some ways he hated himself.

He remembered the balcony, the moment. He could still feel his hand move.

His father's eyes were bloodshot with anger and once more he said, "How could you? My mother! Your grandmother! How could you?"

THE END

EPILOGUE

Sitting in his home office, Arthur Smith watched as some washed-up idiotic shock jock told the world everything. All the secrets Arthur had spent his whole life keeping came out all at once. Clips and proof were being shared online already.

It wasn't like before when they could just cover it up or make excuses. This was too much. There was too much truth and too many wrongs. The people, those fucking people all over the earth, would hate him. They would hate the company. They wouldn't see that what ThutoCo did had kept them alive, kept the planet alive and the colonists alive.

They would just see the lies. See those zealots he had kept in the wastes. See the company's trial run practice with the poison.

He was immobilized with rage even as he knew he had to do something.

His eyes drifted down to the picture of his ex and children. He plucked it off his desk and shook his head. He didn't know why he kept it. She was a bitch. She was the reason he had wanted to do everything he had done.

It was all her fault.

He had made these choices because she had walked away. Taken his children away. Shamed him in front of the world. Those other executives had snickered behind his back. Talked about his failed marriage.

They made those condescending comments right to his face.

He could feel his blood boil, feel the rage growing within him.

It was always there. For years, it had always been there.

He hated that fucking bitch of an ex-wife. Hated the people he worked with. Hated the people who worked for him — all those idiots who had a safe life because of him and would now think him the villain.

It was absurd. They wouldn't see the truth and never could.

They didn't deserve the lives they had. They didn't deserve any life at all.

The time had come.

Stubbing out his cigar on the picture of the people who had been his family, he stood and walked over to the bookshelf, pulling on his copy of *The Price of a Life*. The false book opened a latch and the segment swung open. It was still a small thing that made him happy. He had seen it in movies as he had tried to escape the smell of South African cow shit growing up. Now, as an adult, having a hidden passageway behind a bookshelf was a small luxury that made him smile when so few things did.

Of course, in this moment, nothing could make him smile. He stepped into the narrow passage and through to the room where he had started taking his clandestine calls. The hallway was dimly lit with no adornments.

His palm rang again and he ignored it again. The company he had hired to deal with Moss had failed as spectacularly as Carcer had. As his own Zetas had. The ineptitude surrounding him was staggering. He kept throwing money at people and all of them failed. Again and again. He had gotten close with the breakers, hacking that chip and trying to infect the kid, but even that had ultimately gone nowhere.

And worse, he was blamed for it. These other AIC members made him feel like Moss was his fault. The new mayor was his fault. They blamed him as though their own oppressions didn't contribute to the way the world felt about all of them. It was absurd. He was the one working to help them, to make them kings of the earth, and yet just like those managers they mocked him. They belittled him and acted superior.

Alice Carcer had even had him demoted. At least she was dead now, as was her little lapdog of a warden. That prick who had beaten Arthur was still alive but wouldn't be for long.

Derek, it now seemed, had been a snake in the grass the whole time. That little prick who Arthur had already loathed turned out to be a liar. Everyone was a liar. Every person was a self-interested asshole.

Arthur wanted to spit.

Placing his hand on the pad, it scanned him and the door opened, immediately dialing the other members of the AIC. He had told them to be ready for his call, and soon the room was filled with holoprojected versions of them.

"I am done with this planet," he announced and watched as many nodded. They had been waiting for this day. Many of them impatiently. These people were rich but all of them wanted to be richer. None of them shied from the cost.

That was the one thing that truly united the members of this council: sociopathy. It had taken a long time for Arthur to come to that understanding. When he had abandoned his own family back in Africa and sold his interests in its company to accept the position at ThutoCo, Arthur's brother had flown into a rage.

"You piece of garbage," he had screamed, heartbreak and betrayal written all over his face. Arthur could remember the moment perfectly: the way the light was hitting Table Mountain over his brother's shoulder, the smell from the perfume sprayers set all around the house designed to cover the smell of cow feces and his brother's words. "You are a damned sociopath."

The word had sent Arthur off the deep end, and he had lunged at his brother until he stopped himself and turned to leave. He would have pushed him from the balcony but didn't want to prove his brother right. So he left, feeling nothing but rage.

As the car pulled into the sky, he looked up the definition and smiled.

It was true.

He was a sociopath. Not the serial killer type, but the successful type. The kind a lack of empathy made more successful. He had always had a sense of himself but unlocking this one small thing made him feel as if he *knew* himself.

Looking at the faces in the room and knowing what they had all agreed on, he knew they were like him. Many had families and played at being kind; nearly all of them had charities and foundations in their honor. Arthur himself had several, as well as a scholarship program. He hated having to meet those children every year. There was an annual gala that he was required to attend to keep up appearances. But when he had to meet them, shake their hands, it made him want to be sick.

These people and their ill-fitting suits, mooching off him for something that they could earn themselves, were disgusting. He always noticed the little specks of dirt under their fingernails or bruises on their exposed flesh or tattoos creeping out from under their collars. And they always smelled. It rankled his nose just to think about it. It didn't matter that they had come straight from a bath; they always smelled like poor.

Arthur was happy to be done with them. Happy to be done with all of them.

"How long does everybody need?" he asked.

None of them needed much time. Most of them were ready to begin within a week.

"I will of course begin with B.A. City, but I will begin shipping supplies to all of you so that you may follow suit," he said. It would have to do for now. His city was the one that would give the most resistance, so he was pleased not to give them the chance.

More than anything, he was sick of Moss. He was sick of hearing the name, sick of the implications and sick of his pissant revolution. These children thought they were fighting to save this planet and they had no idea that the wheels were already in motion.

They kept fighting, and Arthur had to admit winning. But it didn't matter. All the battles ThutoCo had lost amounted to nothing because the war had already been won before Moss even began his fight.

And that's what the world would truly see.

Now it was time for the AIC to finally answer. They had waited long enough. Now, earth would become little more than a factory to feed the off-worlders. They would kill all the useless peasants who were little more than drains on the planet's resources and replace them with drudges.

Arthur couldn't help but laugh. When all was said and done, Moss's father's technology would be what made it possible to entirely eradicate the revolution that the man had helped to begin.

Without the senior Scott's personality mapping, the AIs would never have advanced enough to make this possible. Deep learning was one thing, but without being melded with the human mind's creative problem-solving, it was still machine thinking. Now, thanks to Moss and his family, they would be able to rid the entire planet of the human pestilence that plagued it.

"My friends," Arthur said, genuinely elated, "at the beginning of next week we will be the richest people on the planet and by the end of it, we will be the richest people in the galaxy."

A satisfied smile crossed his lips.

This was the end. Not just for Moss and his little friends, but for everyone; and Arthur could watch it on his screens from the safety of his own home. It was perfect.

NOTE TO THE READER

Thanks for reading *Cracked Screens: A Cyberpunk Saga (Book 6)*. If you enjoyed the book, please leave a review; it is incredibly helpful to new authors. Reviews are one of the ways in which people can discover new work and help me to create more of it. Thanks again for reading.

For free content, a glossary of terms, cosplay, concept art and much more, visit Thutoworld.com

AUTHOR BIO

Matthew A. Goodwin has been writing about spaceships, dragons and adventures since he was a child. After creating his first fantasy world at twelve years old, he never stopped writing. Storytelling happened only in the background for over a decade as he spent his days caring for wildlife as a zookeeper, but when his son was born, he decided to pursue his lifelong dream of becoming an author.

Having always loved sweeping space operas and gritty cyberpunk stories that asked questions about man's relationship to technology, he penned the international bestselling series, A Cyberpunk Saga. His passion for the genre also inspired him to create and cofound Cyberpunk Day ™, a celebration of all things high tech / low life.

He is now expanding his science fiction universe into space.

Made in the USA
Las Vegas, NV
26 December 2022

64193757R00136